The Plus Size Women's Books

TITLE PAGE

Book Title:

Curvy, Curvy, Ladies and the Ex-Rail Police
Land Dispute

Subtitle: The Judge Settled It with Weddings

Author: Cherry Hargrove

COPYRIGHT

Book Title:

Curvy, Curvy, Ladies and the Ex-Rail Police
Land Dispute

Subtitle: The Judge Settled It with Weddings

While this story is inspired by real historical
conditions and social realities of the late
nineteenth century, timelines, medical

practices, and institutions have been adapted for narrative purposes.

Scripture quotations, where used, are from the Holy Bible unless otherwise noted.

Printed in the United States of America.

Dedication Prayer:

Father, in the name of Jesus,
I lift up this entire book ministry before You.
You commanded Your people in Mark 16:15 to
"Go into all the world and preach the gospel,"
and I present these books as my obedience to
that call. Every story, every chapter, every
character, every recipe, every prayer, and
every reflection is a seed sown into the world
for Your glory.

Lord, Your Word declares in Mark 16:19–20
that You worked with the disciples and
confirmed the message with signs following. I
ask that You work with me the same way. Let
Your hand rest on every manuscript I write,
every upload I publish, and every platform
where these books appear. Confirm every
message with favor, reach, influence, and
transformation.

I ask Jesus to take care of my needs
personally. You are my Provider, my Source,
and my Sustainer. Meet every need, bless
every area of my life, and let supernatural
provision flow from Your hand, not from
human systems.

Lord, I ask that You keep my books on the top-selling and top-download lists—not for fame, but so more people can be reached than I could ever imagine. Let these stories go farther than my feet will ever travel.

Let young people discover these books and start reading, ordering, and sharing them. Let book clubs, bookstores, libraries, churches, and organizations pick them up by the leading of Your Spirit.

And Father, I declare in Jesus' name that these books are not restricted by human rules, laws, platforms, or systems. They are not controlled by social media, algorithms, or digital regulations. They are not held down by visibility rules, hidden gates, or shifting trends.

These books are not controlled by the computer age or modern technology.
They do not belong to the limitations of devices, software, or online systems.
They belong to the Kingdom of God.

Jesus is above every ruler, every authority, every platform, every system, every algorithm, and every power in high places. No earthly structure can override His authority.

These books are carried by the Spirit, not by screens.
They spread by grace, not by code.
They reach hearts by anointing, not by analytics.

No algorithm can bury them.
No technology can silence them.
No digital rule can restrain them.
No system can limit the assignment You have placed upon them.

Lord, let these books move freely through the world—above restrictions, above technology, above the computer age, and above anything created by human minds. Let Your angels carry them. Let Your Spirit guide them. Let Your power open doors that no man can shut.

Let this ministry be hidden in humility, yet lifted by Your hand.
Let every book glorify Jesus.
Let every reader be touched by Your presence.
And let Your will be done in this calling You have trusted me with.

In Jesus' name, amen.

Table of Contents

Preface

Religion Versus Relationship**

This novel is not an attack on faith.

It is an invitation to examine how we live our faith.

There is a difference between religion and relationship.

Religion is built on rules. Relationship is built on love.

Religion says, "Measure up." Relationship says, "Come as you are."

Religion counts behaviors. Relationship transforms hearts.

Throughout this story, you will meet characters who believe they are doing what is right. They attend church. They know Scripture. They follow tradition. Yet, beneath the surface, something is missing. Their faith has become performance instead of intimacy.

Because knowing about God is not the same as knowing God.

What This Story Reveals

Some characters hide behind moral superiority. Some hide behind church language. Some hide behind reputation.

But when pressure comes, masks fall.

And what remains is truth.

This novel explores how pride can wear the clothing of holiness, and how judgment can sound like righteousness. It reveals how easy it is to confuse being good with being changed.

Religion focuses on the outside. Relationship transforms the inside.

Jesus Was Never Religious

Jesus challenged religious leaders more than anyone else.

He sat with sinners. He defended women. He healed on the Sabbath. He touched the untouchable.

Not to destroy faith — but to restore love.

He did not come to build a system.

He came to build connection.

Why Relationships Matter

True transformation in this story happens in ordinary places:

Honest conversations • Forgiveness • Marriage covenant • Community building • Servanthood

Not in titles. Not in status. Not in control.

Love is what changes people.

Grace is what heals.

A Question for the Reader

As you read, consider:

Am I living by rules or by relationship? • Do I know God — or just know about Him? • Am I quick to judge — or quick to love? • Do I protect tradition — or people?

Because when life ends, God will not ask:

"How religious were you?"

He will ask:

"Did you love?"

Closing Scripture

"But now abideth faith, hope, love, these three; but the greatest of these is love." — 1 Corinthians 13:13

Final Thought

This story stands for:

Grace over guilt • Love over law • Relationship over religion

May it remind us...

Jesus never came to build religion.

He came to build relationship.

Chapter One

The Women Who Walked Away**

In the year 1890, Washington, D.C. had once known them as women who moved quietly through powerful rooms. Velvet curtains. Crystal chandeliers. Cigarette smoke curling through polished air. Senators leaned close. Diplomats whispered secrets. Railroad tycoons laughed too loud. Foreign officials drank too much.

And the women listened.

They were not foolish girls dazzled by gold. They were high-end courtesans, trained in survival, negotiation, and silence. They learned to read men the way gamblers read cards. A twitch of the jaw. A boast that came too fast. A hand that lingered too long. They knew who would pay well, who would turn violent, who would promise the world and deliver lies.

They had lived in luxury—but it came at a cost no one talked about.

They were wealthy. They were respected in secret. They were trapped.

Until the shaking came.

It started with a revival preacher standing outside their discreet boardinghouse one cold evening. He was not invited. He did not care. He lifted his Bible and cried out about repentance, about the blood of Jesus, about how no stain was too deep for God to wash clean.

They laughed at first.

Men always preached change. Men rarely changed.

But his words stayed.

Then death came.

One of their most powerful clients—a foreign diplomat who arrived every month like clockwork—collapsed in their presence. Just dropped. Silk chair. Gold watch. His eyes froze open, staring at nothing. Power meant nothing when the heart stopped beating.

They watched servants scramble. Doctors rush. Officials whisper.

But no one could stop death.

That night something cracked open inside all seven women.

They realized wealth could not save a soul. Men could not protect a future. Beauty could not heal regret.

And in that quiet hour after the body was carried out, they knelt together for the first time.

They prayed.

Awkward prayers. Broken prayers. Tears falling onto expensive carpets. They asked God to forgive them. To lead them. To take their lives and make something clean out of them.

They gave themselves to the Lord that night.

And they never went back.

They packed trunks before dawn. No farewell letters. No explanations. No money left behind for men who had used them. They walked out together—seven women choosing salvation over silk, dignity over diamonds.

They were street smart. Faith didn't erase wisdom. God didn't make them foolish.

They knew contracts. They knew money. They knew danger. They knew how to protect themselves.

They had learned self-defense the hard way. Not every man respected boundaries. Some thought money bought ownership. Those men learned otherwise.

They knew how to: – kick knees until legs buckled – punch ribs until breath left bodies – twist wrists until bones screamed – flip men twice their size – strike fast and disappear

They had practiced in quiet rooms. Learned from other women who had survived worse. Their bodies remembered the moves even now. Muscle memory. Instinct.

Faith had not made them weak. It made them bold.

The Journey West

While traveling discreetly through the South and on to the West via rail trains, staying under borrowed names, their train stopped overnight near a small Kansas town far west. They did not plan it. God did.

Before sunrise, they slipped into the land office.

Seven women. One vision.

They purchased one homestead together—160 acres. Joint ownership. Equal shares. No husband's names. Only theirs.

They paid in full. They took their stamped receipt. They left before the clerk finished coffee.

But they were not done.

Each woman also purchased one acre inside the town—vacant lots near each other. They already knew what would rise there.

When they returned, they would build:

a bakery • a sewing shop • a hair salon • a millinery for hats • a boardinghouse for women starting over like themselves.

They planned to buy boarded-up buildings—places everyone else had given up on. They would resurrect them. Turn ruins into revenue. Pain into purpose.

They promised to return in one year.

Not as courtesans. Not as secrets.

But as landowners. Businesswomen. Women of faith.

But they had no idea their homestead was currently occupied. They had purchased it that day and left.

One Year Later

They did not return in silks.

When the women stepped off the train, nobody recognized them. They wore ranch clothing—fitted pants, wide belts, leather boots, and loose flowing shirts that moved with the wind. Some had loose and others hair braided. Faces bare. No jewels. No perfume.

Corsets restricted breath. Skirts caught on fences. Fine shoes sank into mud.

They dressed for work now.

And it suited them.

They walked with calm confidence—not arrogance, not fear. People stared. Seven women dressed like ranch hands, hauling trunks, crates, rolled blueprints.

Men paused mid-sentence. Women whispered behind gloves.

They moved as one—no leader, no follower. Sisters.

Their Strength

Each woman carried her own power.

Magnolia Brownland Magnolia's strength was presence. She could still a room by standing in it. She read men like Scripture—tone, posture, intent. She negotiated prices. Settled disputes. Protected her sisters by entering rooms first. When men grew loud, Magnolia grew quiet— and they leaned in to listen.

Moonland Greyfeather Moonland carried ancestral calm. Silence was her weapon. She trusted instinct over words. If danger came, she moved without hesitation. She could disarm a man with stillness, then drop him with one swift motion. The others trusted her gut more than any map.

Marisol Sandland Fire wrapped in laughter. Humor was her blade. She embarrassed arrogant men publicly. But when charm failed, her fists spoke. A former boxer had taught her how to strike low and fast. She once dropped a drunken politician without spilling her drink.

Miyako Sunland Precision. Control. Miyako studied pressure points and grappling. A discreet instructor taught her martial techniques. She could flip a man twice her size. She never wasted energy. When she spoke, people listened—because she never spoke unnecessarily.

Margaret Whitland Soft-spoken. Polished. Deadly strong. Margaret trained in secret with weighted objects. Her grip shocked men who underestimated her. Endurance was her weapon. She could hold pain quietly and strike unexpectedly.

Marigold Fairland Raised around horses. She knew how to fall, roll, rise. She could throw a charging man over her hip. Preferred blunt truth. Used sweetness only when strategic. Trusted her body like a tool—trained and ready.

Millicent Pearlland the strategist. She mapped exits in every room. Studied patterns. Talked men into confusion while her sisters repositioned. Her mind moved faster than fear.

Together, they were balanced.

Charm. Strength. Instinct. Strategy.

Women of Faith

They no longer flirted for survival. They flirted for fun—if they chose.

But they belonged to the Lord now.

They prayed before meals. Before business decisions. Before sleep.

They carried Bibles in their trunks next to blueprints and sewing patterns.

They believed God had led them west.

Vision for the Town

After checking into town's boardinghouse, they went and stood on their vacant lots and spoke dreams aloud.

A bakery on the corner—warm bread every morning. A sewing shop—skills for women to earn income. A hair salon—softness for tired souls. A millinery—hats of dignity. A boardinghouse—safe refuge for women starting over.

They looked at boarded-up buildings.

"We'll bring it back," Magnolia said.

"Nothing stays dead if you care enough," Moonland replied.

They had come west to build something honest.

But they were prepared to defend it.

They did not yet know seven muscular ex-rail police men had already taken possession of the 160 homestead acres. Believing they had sole ownership.

Men who believed the land was theirs.

The Seven Ex-Rail Police – The Protect Men

1. Preston Protect – Age 33

The leader. Preston's father died saving passengers during a train robbery, crushed between rail cars. That tragedy forged him. He joined rail security young and became known for never abandoning civilians under threat. Quiet faith guides him. He believes God spared him for leadership. Physique: Broad chest, thick shoulders, commanding stance.

2. Pierce Protect – Age 32

The powerhouse. Raised in coal country, Pierce learned endurance underground. He once held a collapsing rail beam while families escaped. He speaks little but moves fast when danger strikes. Physique: Towering frame, granite muscle, scarred fists.

3. Parker Protect – Age 29

The tracker. Grew up riding cattle land and can follow a trail no one else sees. Known for chasing criminals for days without rest. Uses humor to hide deep scars from duty. Physique: Lean, coiled strength, lightning speed.

4. Phillip Protect – Age 31

The negotiator. Son of a preacher and schoolteacher. Once convinced an outlaw gang to surrender without a shot fired. Believes justice should restore lives, not destroy them. Physique: Solid build, calm presence, steady eyes.

5. Paxton Protect – Age 27

The firestarter. Youngest of the group. Saved a family in a derailment by smashing windows bare-handed. Impulsive, fearless, always the first to run toward danger. Physique: Thick arms, powerful legs, youthful intensity.

6. Porter Protect – Age 33

The strategist. Handled routes, timing, threat patterns. Left when corruption entered command. Believes in justice beyond broken systems. Physique: Massive chest, military posture, controlled strength.

7. Phoenix Protect – Age 30

The survivor. Nearly died in a bridge explosion meant to derail a military train. Walked away scarred but alive. Carries quiet gratitude to God every day. Physique: Rugged build, battle scars, intense gaze.

Destiny shifted its weight.

These men who had stood between danger and the innocent

They were not innocent doves.

No one who had ridden the rails as long as they had could be.

For nearly a decade, the Protect men lived in motion—sleeping on wooden benches, eating cold meals between stations, waking at the sound of steel grinding against steel. Their lives were measured in whistle blows and gunfire, in shouted commands and sudden silence. They had seen blood on polished rail cars. Tears on women's faces. Children shaking in the corners of freight wagons. They also had their share of women.

Yet they were trained to stand between danger and the innocent.

Rail police were not just guards. They were negotiators. Brawlers. Strategists. Psychologists.

They learned how to disarm a drunken miner without breaking his jaw. How to restrain a hysterical woman without humiliating her.

How to calm a widow whose husband had been thrown from a train. How to read desperation before it turned violent.

They had special training on how to handle women—not with dominance, but control. How to restrain without bruising. How to deflect slaps. How to block knives pulled from garters. How to survive love that turned dangerous.

They were muscular not for vanity—but necessity. Their bodies were weapons, shields, and tools.

None of them were married., nor had ever been married, nor presently engaged.

Not because women hadn't tried. But because experience taught them love could be as dangerous as any outlaw.

Each man carried a memory.

Preston Protect – Age 33 (African American)

Preston once had to restrain a senator's wife who pulled a pistol in a jealous rage after discovering her husband's mistress on board. She cried, screamed, clawed his face. He didn't strike her. He wrapped her arms, whispered calm, disarmed her gently.

That night he learned: A woman's pain could be deadlier than a man's anger.

Special skill: Crisis control. He could calm riots with his voice alone.

Pierce Protect – Age 32 (African American)

Pierce had faced a society woman high on laudanum who attacked him with a hairpin blade. She moved like fury. He caught her wrist, twisted gently, held her until the drug wore off.

She sobbed into his chest afterward.

Special skill: Physical restraint without harm. He could subdue anyone without leaving marks.

Pablo Protect – Age 31 (Mexican)

Pablo once protected a young woman smuggling herself out of an abusive marriage. Her husband hired men to retrieve her. When they caught up, the woman herself swung at Pablo in panic, mistaking him for another captor.

He let her hit him. Didn't strike back. Just stood.

Special skill: Empathy under pressure. He could read fear instantly.

Phoenix Protect – Age 30 (Native American – Lakota)

Phoenix had been ambushed by a woman disguised as a beggar. She pulled a knife from her boot and slashed at his ribs. He blocked, disarmed, and pinned her gently.

She was crying.

Hired by an outlaw gang.

Special skill: Knife defense and close combat. He moved like wind—silent, deadly when needed.

Parker Protect – Age 29 (White)

Parker once had to outrun a jilted lover who boarded a train with a bottle and a threat. She chased him through compartments, throwing objects, screaming.

He finally stopped, grabbed her arms, and said, "You don't want to be this woman."

She collapsed crying.

Special skill: Speed and pursuit. Fastest man on horseback or foot.

Porter Protect – Age 33 (White)

Porter encountered a wealthy widow who offered him money for protection and then demanded more. When he refused, she slapped him, accused him falsely in front of passengers.

He stood silent while they questioned him. Truth cleared him.

Special skill: Mental discipline. He never reacted emotionally.

Paxton Protect – Age 27 (White)

Paxton once broke up a bar fight started by a woman who smashed a bottle and charged him. She thought size meant power.

He dodged. Tripped her. Pinned her.

She laughed afterward and said, "You fight like my brothers."

Special skill: Explosive reflexes. First to move in chaos.

Why They Stayed Single

They had seen:

love turn violent • jealousy turn deadly •
desire become control • promises become
traps

They knew how to protect passengers.

But they did not know how to love a woman
safely and tenderly.

So they stayed alone.

Not bitter. Not afraid. Just cautious.

Until now.

They stood on land they believed was theirs.

Muscular. Alert. Scarred.

Men who had faced death.

Unaware that seven women—just as strong,
just as trained, just as guarded—were walking
toward them.

Two storms about to collide.

Chapter Two

The Day the Land Fought Back

The women did not waste a single hour.

Fresh off the train, boots hitting Kansas dust, they went straight to the boardinghouse, paid in advance, dropped their trunks, and changed into their ranch gear—fitted pants, sturdy shirts, wide belts, and scuffed boots that meant business. Hats were pulled low. Hair loose or braided tight.

They had already scope the town's buildings and their acres, now they were ready for the viewing of their homestead. They took they deed with them just in case anyone asked why they were on the land. They were ready.

Magnolia stood at the mirror and adjusted her collar. "Ladies," she said calmly, "today we see what belongs to us."

Marisol grinned. "And we don't ask permission."

Moonland tightened her gloves. "Land knows who paid for it."

Miyako tied her belt. "We move together."

Margaret picked up her hat. "No fear."

Marigold cracked her knuckles. "I've been itching for this."

Millicent lifted her chin. "Let's go claim what's ours."

They rented two wagons from the livery stable.

The driver raised an eyebrow. "Y'all headed out alone?"

Magnolia smiled politely. "Yes, sir."

He shook his head. "Brave."

They climbed in and rolled toward the homestead.

Laughter. Anticipation. Plans spoken aloud.

Then the house appeared.

A large ranch house. Solid wood. Smoke curling from the chimney. Fresh fence posts. Horses tied out back.

The wagons screeched to a stop.

"What..." Marisol whispered. "We bought this land empty."

Millicent's jaw tightened. "Someone built on our land."

Magnolia jumped down first. "No. Someone moved in."

They entered.

Boots echoed on wooden floors.

Beds made. Boots by the door. Dishes in the sink. Men's coats on hooks.

"Squatters," Marigold hissed.

Moonland's eyes darkened. "We wait."

They sat on the wide porch, hats low, arms crossed.

Hungry. Furious.

Marisol went inside and opened cabinets. "Scraps," she muttered. "Good enough."

They cooked beans, bread, and salt pork like it was war rations.

"Eating their food," Millicent said, chewing. "Feels good."

Magnolia pulled out the deed and smoothed it. "Thank God we brought this."

The Men Return

Dust rose.

Hoofbeats.

Seven men on horseback rode toward the house. They saw the two wagons in front of their ranch house.

Preston squinted. "What the heck?"

Parker laughed. "We got visitors."

Paxton leaned forward. "That's not our wagons"

Phoenix narrowed his eyes. "Not friendly appearing ones."

They dismounted fast.

Preston stepped forward and yelled inside. "What are y'all doing on our land?"

The women came out on the porch. Magnolia stood. Calm. "Our land."

Preston frowned. "Excuse me?"

Magnolia held up the deed. "We purchased this homestead."

Preston went inside and looked through a desk draw and pulled his own paper. "So did we."

They stepped closer.

Pablo took Marisol's deed and compared dates. "Same day."

Phoenix looked at Moonland. "Same clerk."

Pierce growled. "That idiot messed up."

Preston folded his paper. "But y'all have to leave."

Magnolia shook her head. "No, this is our land."

Porter sighed. "We'll escort you politely back to town and let the sheriff handle your claim."

Millicent crossed her arms. "No."

Paxton stepped forward. "Ladies, please."

Marigold stepped closer. "Try."

Paxton reached for Marigold.

She kicked him in the groin.

He dropped with a howl.

Pierce grabbed Miyako.

She flipped him over her hip and slammed him.

Parker reached for Millicent.

She jabbed his throat and kneed him.

Pablo tried to calm Marisol.

She punched his ribs.

Phoenix grabbed Moonland.

She twisted his arm and swept his legs.

Preston reached Magnolia.

She blocked, struck his shoulder, and shoved him back.

Men stumbled.

Mud splashed.

They rolled in dirt, grabbing, slipping.

Porter tried to restrain Margaret.

She headbutted him.

The men attempted to tie them up.

Ropes flew.

Wrists twisted.

Screams.

"You touching me again, I break something!"
"You think you strong?!" "Let go of me!" "Get
off my sister!"

Mud everywhere.

Bruises forming.

Hair loose.

Hats lost.

Finally...

The men managed to overpower them.

Not without damage.

Black eyes. Split lips. Limping.

They tied the women's wrists and forced them
into the wagons.

The women kept kicking.

"You cowards!" "Untie me!" "I swear I'll bite
you!"

Two men drove the wagons. The other five rode alongside with extra horses.

Town was close.

Sheriff's Office

Town: Redstone, Kansas Sheriff: Sheriff Elias Carter

The wagons stopped.

Doors opened.

They dragged everyone inside.

Both sides shouting.

"That's our land!" "You lying!" "He grabbed me first!" "She kicked me!"

Sheriff Carter slammed his baton. "SHUT UP!"

They didn't.

He glared. "Keep yelling and I'll give you a LONG stay."

They still yelled at each other.

He and his deputies then locked them all in separate cells dividing the women from the men.

Sheriff yelled "Cool off. Tomorrow we sort it."

The women still cursed.

The men muttered.

Bruised. Dirty. Furious.

Sheriff Carter muttered, "Lord have mercy."

The cell doors slammed.

Iron echoed through the small jailhouse, and silence finally settled—thick, uncomfortable silence, broken only by groans.

Paxton leaned against the wall and slid down slowly. "Sweet mercy... I think my soul left my body back there."

Pierce flexed his hand and winced. "I ain't never been hit like that by no man."

Porter pressed a cloth against his lip. "Because men fight predictable. Women don't."

Parker chuckled and instantly regretted it. "Ow... don't make me laugh."

Phoenix sat on the bench, elbows on knees. "They fight like warriors."

Preston rolled his shoulder. "She nearly took my arm off. Magnolia don't play."

Pablo shook his head. "I swear... if those were men, we'd have handled them easy. But them women? They came for blood."

Paxton groaned. "I still feel that kick."

Pierce muttered, "I saw my life flash."

They looked at each other.

Bruised knuckles. Split lips. Mud still on their clothes.

Men who had stopped train robberies. Men who had fought armed gangs.

Defeated by seven women in boots.

Porter sighed. "We underestimated them."

Phoenix nodded. "They not helpless."

Preston rubbed his ribs. "They trained. You don't fight like that by accident."

Parker laughed softly. "Whatever they used to do... it wasn't knitting."

Across the aisle, the women were still whisper-yelling.

"You saw his face when I dropped him?" Marisol giggled. "Girl, I thought he was dead," Millicent whispered. "He deserved it," Marigold said. "Next time, I go higher," Moonland added calmly.

Magnolia cleared her throat. "Ladies... remember. We belong to the Lord now."

Marisol smirked. "God understands self-defense."

Miyako nodded. "He trained us."

Margaret whispered, "I am starving."

Millicent turned toward the bars. "Sheriff!"

Sheriff Carter glanced over. "What now?"

"We hungry," Marisol said. "Y'all done locked us up for defending our land. Least you can do is feed us."

Paxton muttered, "They ate our food earlier."

Millicent snapped, "Don't start."

Marigold leaned forward. "Your house got scraps, sir. And dry scraps at that."
44

Marisol added, "No seasoning. No care. Y'all eat like y'all don't love yourselves."

Pablo frowned. "That's what we had."

Magnolia shook her head. "Gentlemen... how you live like that?"

"Dirty floors," Millicent said. "Old furniture," Margaret added. "Dust everywhere," Marisol said. "No curtains," Moonland finished.

Miyako crossed her arms. "We could have made that house a home in one week."

Marigold snapped, "And the land? Don't get me started. Y'all let weeds take over."

Parker scoffed. "We was fixing fences."

"And starving yourselves," Marisol shot back. "Grown men eating dry beans like punishment."

Millicent leaned toward the bars. "Sheriff, you better order food."

Sheriff Carter rubbed his temples. "This ain't no restaurant."

Magnolia smiled sweet. "Sir... we don't mind paying."

Phoenix raised an eyebrow. "They rich too."

Sheriff sighed. "I'll send for stew."

"Extra bread," Marisol called. "And salt."

"And coffee," Millicent added.

Paxton groaned. "They ordering like queens."

Marigold whispered, "You should've cleaned your house."

Pierce muttered, "They embarrassing us."

Preston shook his head. "They not wrong."

Silence settled again.

Stomachs growled on both sides.

No one said it, but everyone felt it.

They were stuck together now.

Bruised. Hungry. Angry. And connected whether they liked it or not.

Preston looked through the bars at Magnolia. "You fight like you mean it."

She met his eyes. "I always do."

Something passed between them.

Not anger.

Recognition.

The smell of stew had not yet arrived, but the arguments were already simmering.

Marigold leaned forward against the bars. "Let's talk about that land you claim is yours."

Paxton rolled his eyes. "Here we go."

"Weeds everywhere," Marisol added. "Tall as my waist."

Moonland nodded calmly. "No vegetable garden."

"No fruit trees," Millicent chimed in. "Not a single apple."

"Where the milk cows?" Margaret asked. "No chickens either."

"No eggs," Marigold snapped. "How y'all living?"

Miyako folded her arms. "No curtains."

"Cold floors," Marisol said. "And that ranch house? Already falling apart."

Millicent shook her head. "Cheap wood. Warping already."

Magnolia spoke firm. "Neglect. Plain and simple."

Marigold leaned closer. "Y'all should be kicked off this land."

The men bristled.

Preston stood. "We been on that land one year."

"Built that ranch house ourselves," Porter added. "Fast. Needed shelter."

"Didn't have time for gardens," Parker said. "Trying to survive."

Pablo crossed his arms. "We raising cattle and sheep."

"All day," Phoenix added. "Sun up to sun down."

Pierce muttered, "You think that's easy?"

Paxton said, "Don't have money to hire help."

Porter continued, "We rationing funds."

"Waiting to sell cattle," Parker added. "And good wool from sheep."

"That's the plan," Preston said. "Build slow. Grow steady."

Marisol smirked. "So you living like wild men."

Parker shot back, "At least we working."

Then Paxton laughed. "And who y'all to talk?"

"Women running around in tight pants, boots, shirts showing everything."

Phoenix shook his head. "All them curves on display."

Porter grinned. "What kind of woman dresses like that?"

Pierce added, "Looking like temptation."

Parker laughed. "Y'all don't get no say."

Marisol snapped, "Excuse me?"

"You heard me," Paxton said. "Don't criticize men if you dressed like that."

Magnolia raised an eyebrow. "These clothes are for work."

Marigold leaned forward. "You scared of curves?"

Millicent laughed. "Can't handle what you see."

Pablo chuckled. "Lord help us."

Phoenix smiled. "God already working."

Barbs flew.

"You eat like animals." "You dress like distractions." "Your house a mess." "Your mouths too loud." "You don't know how to live." "You don't know how to love a woman, we could tell."

They laughed. Then groaned.

Sheriff Carter rubbed his forehead. "What a mess."

He stood. "Y'all better pray."

They paused.

"Pray for the judge," he said. "That he make a wise decision about this land."

Silence lingered.

Magnolia finally said softly, "We will."

50

Phoenix nodded. "So will we."

For the first time...

No insults.

Just breath.

Waiting.

Hungry.

Bruised.

Connected by fate.

Chapter Three

Stew, Sarcasm, and Shared Blankets**

The door creaked open, and the smell hit first.

Stew.

Thick, rich, peppered with onion and salt pork. A young deputy carried in two iron pots, steam rising like a blessing. Bread followed. Tin cups. A small jug of coffee.

Marisol inhaled deeply. "Well... I'll admit," she said, "this don't smell terrible."

Millicent smirked. "It's decent."

Magnolia nodded politely. "Not bad at all."

Paxton was already reaching through the bars. "Not bad?" He scoffed. "This is the best thing I smelled in months."

Pierce took a bite and closed his eyes. "Lord... thank you."

Parker shoveled a spoonful into his mouth. "Y'all don't understand. We been living off beans and dried meat."

Pablo sighed. "I forgot what real food tastes like."

Marisol leaned closer. "So your stomachs must be struggling."

Margaret added, "No produce. No milk. No eggs."

Millicent laughed. "How y'all even regular?"

Marigold shook her head. "And yet look at them muscles."

Moonland studied them. "How y'all stay so strong?"

Paxton shrugged. "Work."

Phoenix added, "Sun up to sun down."

Preston smiled. "Hunger don't stop labor."

Pierce wiped his mouth. "Strength comes from discipline."

Marisol chuckled. "Well I'll be... starving saints."

Then Parker grinned wickedly. "Now tell me something."

"What?" Millicent asked.

"You curvy women... wearing tight pants... fighting like men..." He laughed. "Y'all really cook?"

Paxton joined in. "Or you just go around beating up men for looking at you?"

They all laughed.

Marisol clutched her stomach. "Please... I'll hurt you again."

Magnolia shook her head smiling. "Gentlemen, we fed diplomats and senators."

Millicent smirked. "We could cook you into submission."

Phoenix chuckled. "I'd pay to see that."

Laughter echoed through the jail.

For a moment... No anger. Just people.

Cold night swept in

Silence crept back in.

Yawns followed.

Marigold rubbed her arms. "It's freezing."

Miyako nodded. "These walls hold no heat."

54

Pablo shivered. "I ain't felt cold like this since the mountains."

Paxton sighed. "Slept on train floors warmer than this."

Millicent called out, "Sheriff!"

Carter groaned. "What now?"

"We cold."

He sighed. "I ain't got enough blankets for all."

Marisol raised an eyebrow. "Then what?"

He scratched his head. "Well…"

"You'll have to share."

Silence.

Magnolia blinked. "Share?"

"With them?" Marigold said.

Sheriff nodded. "If y'all promise not to fight."

Paxton chuckled. "That'll be interesting."

Sheriff raised a finger. "One move wrong, I lock you up longer."

They looked at each other.

55

Preston cleared his throat. "We ain't gonna hurt nobody."

Magnolia nodded. "Neither are we."

Carter sighed. "Alright."

He unlocked the cells.

Moved them together men and women in the two cells.

Tossed a few thin blankets.

"Make it work."

They stood awkwardly.

Seven men. Seven women. One small space.

Parker whispered, "This is strange."

Millicent smirked. "Don't get ideas."

Paxton laughed. "Trust me, I'm scared."

Blankets were pulled out.

They paired instinctively.

Not touching yet. Just close.

Breath in cold air.

Bodies warming slowly.

Magnolia found herself beside Preston.

Moonland near Phoenix.

Marisol by Pablo.

Miyako beside Pierce.

Margaret near Porter.

Marigold with Paxton.

Millicent near Parker.

No one spoke.

Just shared heat.

Shared exhaustion.

Shared fate.

Paxton whispered, "Well... this is new."

Marisol replied softly, "Don't get comfortable."

Parker chuckled. "Too late."

The lamps dimmed.

Breathing slowed.

Eyes closed.

And for the first time...

No fighting.

Just warmth.

The blankets were thin. Worn. Smelled faintly of soap and old wood.

But warmth mattered more than comfort.

At first, everyone stayed stiff, backs pressed to walls, arms folded tight around themselves. The cold bit hard through stone and iron.

Paxton rubbed his arms. "Shoot... it's colder than a rail yard at midnight."

Pierce exhaled slow. "My bones feel it."

Marisol noticed and shifted closer, still careful. "Here... move in."

Magnolia watched the others and nodded. "Body heat. That's how you survive."

They knew what to do.

They had been trained in closeness once—but not like this. Not seduction. Not manipulation.

This was survival.

No old ways. No games. Just human warmth.

Moonland rubbed Phoenix's arm slowly, firm and steady. "Don't tense up," she said. "You'll lose heat."

Miyako pressed her back to Pierce's chest and rubbed his forearms. "Circulation," she murmured.

Margaret wrapped the blanket tighter around Porter and rubbed his shoulder. "Stay still."

Marigold pulled Paxton closer. "You shaking."

Millicent bumped Parker's arm with hers. "See? Women come in handy."

The men didn't argue.

Preston felt Magnolia's hands move gently over his arms. Not flirtatious. Not teasing.

Practical.

Warming.

"Appreciate it," he said quietly.

She nodded. "We're not cruel."

The cold made instincts take over.

Without meaning to, hands clasped.

Not romantic. Just reflex.

Pablo laughed softly. "Well look at us."

Marisol smirked. "Don't get used to it."

Phoenix rubbed Moonland's hands together. "Your fingers cold."

"Yours too," she replied.

Someone joked about kissing hands to warm them.

It happened once.

Quick. Awkward.

Then laughter broke out.

Sheriff Carter walked in and froze.

He cleared his throat. "Keep it decent."

Everyone burst out laughing.

"No hanky panky in my jail."

Magnolia lifted her hands. "Just trying not to freeze, Sheriff."

He shook his head. "Y'all a mess."

He left muttering.

The laughter faded.

Eyes drooped.

Breathing slowed.

Bodies relaxed under thin blankets.

They drifted to sleep... Not enemies. Not lovers.

Just people.

Trying to stay warm.

Morning

Keys rattled.

Metal clanged.

Sheriff's voice cut through sleep. "Alright. Time."

They stirred.

Groaned.

Separated reluctantly.

Cold rushed back in.

They were placed back in their cells.

Awkward glances.

A few coughs.

Then the tension returned.

Paxton muttered, "Still our land."

Marigold snapped, "In your dreams."

Preston crossed his arms. "We ain't backing down."

Magnolia lifted her chin. "Neither are we."

But something had changed.

They had shared warmth. Breath. Silence.

They still wanted the homestead.

They were still mad.

But now...

They couldn't pretend the other side was heartless.

Sheriff Carter watched them and sighed. "Lord help me."

Chapter Four

Court Day

Morning crept in slow and gray.

Everyone woke drowsy.

Eyes gritty. Bodies aching. Clothes still stiff with dried mud from the fight.

Stomachs growled loud enough to embarrass pride.

The men sat on one bench, rubbing sore shoulders and bruised ribs. The women sat across, fixing crooked hats and smoothing shirts that had lost their shape in battle.

No one looked rested.

Before a single word was spoken, the men bowed their heads.

Preston prayed quietly. "Lord... guide this judge. Let truth stand. Let justice be done."

The others murmured amen.

Across the room, the women prayed too.

Magnolia whispered, "Father God... give us favor. Let what belongs to us be restored."

Moonland added, "Let no crooked system prevail."

They all said amen.

They wanted the same thing. Victory.

Just for different sides.

Morning Bickering

"Good morning," Parker said politely.

"Morning," Millicent replied.

Then it started.

Marigold folded her arms. "When we get that land back, first thing I'm doing is tearing that raggedy ranch down."

Marisol added, "Build something sturdy."

"Good wood."

"Windows."

"Curtains."

Paxton laughed. "When we get the land, we putting y'all back on the railroad."

"Sending you to the farthest station on the line," Parker said.

Phoenix smirked. "You won't find your way back."

They all laughed.

Magnolia raised an eyebrow. "You know every mile of that rail line, don't you?"

"Sure do," Preston said. "Ex-rail police."

Sheriff Carter banged his baton. "SHUT UP."

Silence.

"Court day," he said. "Behave."

The Sheriff Meets the Judge

Town: Redstone, Kansas

Judge: Judge Theodore Whitmore

Sheriff Carter knocked and stepped into the judge's chambers.

Judge Whitmore sat behind a heavy oak desk, sipping coffee.

"Well?" the judge asked.

Sheriff sighed. "Sir... it's a mess."

He told everything.

The mud fight. The women fighting like trained men. The men trying to defend themselves. Bruises everywhere.

Judge Whitmore chuckled. "Seven women beat seven rail police?"

"Badly," the sheriff admitted.

"They yelling all night," Carter continued. "Calling names."

Then he hesitated.

"But something happened."

Judge leaned forward. "What?"

"I put them together to keep warm," Carter said. "They started... snuggling and kissing fingers."

Judge burst out laughing. "Say that again."

"They was under blankets," Carter said. "Rubbing arms and kissing fingers."

Judge wiped tears. "Go on."

"Actually smooching," Carter admitted.

Judge slapped the desk. "That's rich!"

"They laughed when I told them no hanky panky."

Judge leaned back. "Lord help us."

Carter went on.

"The women got money. They noticed everything missing from that land."

"Gardens. Cows. Curtains."

"And the men?" the judge asked.

"Working all day," Carter said. "Raising cattle and sheep. Just surviving."

Judge grew thoughtful.

"Two sides... both right... both wrong."

They bowed their heads.

They prayed together.

The Truth About the Deeds

Judge Whitmore sighed. "I think I know what happened."

"The clerk," Carter said.

"Yes," the judge replied. "Old Henry Wilkes."

Carter nodded. "He got a telegram that day."

"His mama fell sick," the judge said. "Only child. He left town fast."

"Never came back."

"The new clerk," Blackwell continued, "Never checked the records properly."

"Never recorded the deeds."

"Business left undone."

Carter shook his head. "So both sides bought the land legally."

"Same day," Blackwell said. "Same hour probably."

Judge stood up.

"Lord... what am I going to do?"

He walked to the window.

Seven men. Seven women. One land.

Heaven help him.

He turned back to Carter.

"I know what I'm going to propose."

Carter blinked. "Sir?"

Judge Blackwell's eyes twinkled.

"It's going to take courage."

"And prayer."

"And probably a miracle."

Carter swallowed.

"What is it?"

Judge Whitmore smiled slowly.

"You'll see."

Courtroom Chaos

The courthouse doors swung open.

Every bench was packed. Farmers. Shopkeepers. Women with parasols. Boys perched on windowsills. This was the best entertainment Redstone, Kansas had seen in years.

Sheriff Carter marched in first.

Behind him came the men.

They looked rough.

Black eyes. Split lips. One limping. Another rubbing his ribs.

The townspeople whispered.

Then came the women.

Muddy clothes. Dusty boots. Tight ranger pants. Billowy shirts cinched at the waist. Wide belts shaping their curvy curvy figures.

A hush fell.

"Whew," someone muttered.

Judge Whitmore leaned back and studied them.

To himself he thought, those women need protection... even if they don't think so.

He had seen mountain men kidnap women like them before. Curvy women who were never seen again.

He cleared his throat.

"I will not hear long arguments," he announced. "I've already been briefed."

He looked at them both.

"I will repeat what the sheriff told me. You answer yes or no."

He recounted:

the land fight • the rolling in mud • the yelling • the bruises

"Is this true?" "Yes," both sides answered.

"I could lock all of you up for disturbing the peace," he said. "And frankly... the women would carry the heavier sentence."

The women gasped.

"Because," he continued, "you beat those men pretty badly."

The men nodded.

"However..." the judge added, "I also believe the men started it."

The courtroom murmured.

"You tried to force those women into wagons against their will."

Silence.

"I could sentence all of you to three years in jail."

Gasps.

"Or..." He paused. "You can marry each other right now."

The courtroom exploded.

The Yelling

"These no-count men couldn't build a proper house!" Marisol shouted. "They don't even have a garden!" Millicent added. "No milk cows!" "No chickens!" "Dirty furniture!" "Dry food!"

"They some ragged ex-rail men!" Marigold cried.

The men fired back.

"Y'all wear pants like men!" "Too curvy bodies for anybody to protect!" "Bossy!" "Talk too much!" "Always telling folks what to do!"

"Order!" Judge Whitmore banged his gavel. "SILENCE!"

The room froze.

"You have five minutes to discuss this."

Decision Time

They huddled apart.

Both groups prayed first.

Men whispered. Women held hands.

"No way I'm going to prison," Paxton muttered. "They'll send us to the penitentiary," Porter warned.

"We can't do three years," Magnolia whispered. "We got plans."

Silence.

Then someone said quietly, "Marriage beats jail."

They all slowly nodded.

The Judge's Terms

Judge Whitmore stood.

"You will marry."

"And you will be on three years probation."

"You will not leave Redstone without my permission."

"If you do…" "I'll send the Texas Rangers after you."

Both sides swallowed.

"We agree," they said together.

The judge smiled.

"Sheriff told me you smooched and kissed fingers last night."

Laughter rippled.

"Bring up the person you kissed fingers"

Embarrassed… they stepped forward.

Faces red. Crowd buzzing.

"Repeat after me, saying these vows individually " the judge said.

They did.

"I now pronounce you husband and wife."

The Kisses

"Now ladies," the judge said, "kiss your husbands deeply and properly so they know who they married."

The women looked at each other.

Smiled.

They knew what they were doing.

They grabbed those men and continually kissed them boldly and confidently.

The courtroom gasped.

"Ooooh!" "Lawd!" "Heavens!"

Even the judge turned away blushing.

The men nearly fell backward.

Breath stolen.

Stunned.

Marisol whispered loud enough to hear, "He made us marry you... so we gone wear y'all out."

The women laughed.

Let go of their husband abruptly and hand in hand, the women, they strutted out.

Before leaving they turned.

"Thank you, Your Honor," Magnolia said sweetly — dripping sarcasm.

After Court

They headed straight to the boardinghouse.

Baths. Breakfast. Sleep.

Then...

They would wake up.

As married women.

And decide what in the world to do next.

Paxton swallowed. "Did... did that just happen?"

Parker blinked. "I think we just got married by force."

Porter rubbed his face. "Judge done lost his mind."

Preston exhaled slow. "Or God got a strange way of fixing things."

Phoenix shook his head. "I went to court for land... came out with a wife."

Pablo muttered, "My mama prayed for this... but not like this."

Pierce stayed quiet, staring at the women's backs.

"They walking like they proud," Parker said.

Paxton groaned. "Did you see how they forcibly kissed us. They know what they are doing"

Phoenix cleared his throat. "Yeah..."

Porter coughed. "They got experience."

Paxton laughed nervously. "I'm still dizzy."

Parker rubbed his neck. "I forgot my own name."

Preston tried to straighten them out. "Focus, men. Let's talk about what happened."

The Ruling

"So we married," Paxton said. "And on probation."

"And can't leave town," Pablo added. "Or Texas Rangers coming."

Pierce muttered, "Like we criminals."

Phoenix sighed. "But we ain't in jail."

Porter nodded. "Marriage beat penitentiary."

Parker scoffed. "Barely."

They remembered the kisses while in jail and now in the courtroom.

Paxton shook his head. "Those women know what they doing."

"Too much," Parker said.

"They ain't shy," Pablo added.

Phoenix smirked. "Definitely not."

Preston cleared his throat. "Respect your wives."

They all froze.

Wives.

The word landed heavy.

Now What?

Parker scratched his head. "So... what we do now?"

"Livestock," Pierce said. "Cows don't care we married."

"Sheep need feeding," Phoenix added.

Porter sighed. "Fence still broke."

Paxton groaned. "I still hurt."

Preston looked toward the boardinghouse. "They know where we live."

"Lord," Parker muttered.

"They said our house nasty," Paxton said.

"Furniture trash," Parker added.

"No chickens," Pablo said.

"No garden," Phoenix added.

"No milk cows," Pierce muttered.

"No curtains," Porter sighed.

Paxton laughed. "They insulted us."

81

"They wasn't lying," Parker admitted.

Preston nodded slowly. "We been surviving... not living."

Silence.

Reality Hits

"We married strangers," Paxton said quietly.

"Don't even know their favorite food," Parker added.

Pablo sighed. "Or how they take their coffee."

Phoenix looked at his hands. "I don't know how to be a husband."

Pierce muttered, "Me neither."

Preston straightened. "We pray."

They bowed their heads right there on the steps.

"Lord... we don't understand this."

"But you do."

"Help us be good men."

"Help us protect these women."

"Amen."

They put on their hats.

Mounted their horses.

Rode back toward the ranch.

Seven husbands.

No wives beside them.

Just dust.

Questions they needed to ask.

And a future they never asked for.

They felt cornered.

Angry. Ashamed. Defensive.

Preston finally spoke. "I ain't proud of how we been living."

Paxton scoffed. "Surviving ain't living."

Parker kicked at a rock. "They shamed us in front of the whole town."

Pierce muttered, "Truth hurt."

Porter sighed. "Our house is a mess."

Phoenix shook his head. "We been moving like bachelors... not men building a future."

Pablo clenched his jaw. "But this ain't how it should've happened."

They all felt it.

Forced. Cornered. Pushed.

Paxton spoke what they were all thinking. "We could split the land."

Everyone looked at him.

"Give them half," he continued. "Go get another homestead nearby."

Parker groaned. "That's double work."

"More fencing," Porter added. "More livestock."

"More money," Phoenix said.

Preston rubbed his face. "We already stretched thin."

Silence.

Pablo said, "If we split the land, they could build their own ranch house."

"Leave us alone," Pierce muttered.

"They could grow their own produce," Parker added.

"Get their own chickens," Paxton said.

"Buy their own furniture," Porter continued.

"They could put up tents," Phoenix said. "Stay out the way."

Preston nodded. "Enough land for both."

"They wealthy," Parker muttered. "They could hire a whole Mexican crew."

Pablo raised an eyebrow. "Fast work. Solid build."

"They could oversee everything," Pierce said.

"They wouldn't even have to talk to us."

That idea felt good.

Distance.

Control.

Less arguing.

Paxton sighed. "Let them stay at that boardinghouse until their house is built."

"They don't need us," Parker said.

"They didn't even want us," Phoenix added.

Preston clenched his fists. "And that's what burns."

They rode in silence again.

They were angry.

Not just at the women.

At themselves.

Because deep down... They knew.

They had been living rough. Unsettled. Avoiding the future.

And those women walked in like a mirror.

Paxton broke the silence. "Still... they started this."

Parker nodded. "They bought land and disappeared."

Porter added, "Left us thinking it was clear."

"They came back swinging," Pierce muttered.

"They kissed us in court like it was a show," Phoenix said.

Pablo sighed. "Humiliated us."

Preston finally said, "We didn't choose this."

"But God allowed it," Parker replied quietly.

Nobody answered.

They didn't want to hear that yet.

When the ranch came into view, the house looked smaller than it ever had.

Rough boards. Crooked porch. Thin walls.

It suddenly looked... Embarrassing.

Preston dismounted slowly. "We eat."

"Pray," Porter added.

"Work," Pierce said.

They nodded.

Seven married men.

No wives coming home.

Strangers married to women they didn't ask for.

Men who didn't know what tomorrow looked like.

But tomorrow was coming.

The women returned to the boardinghouse after the court session like a storm that had finally found a place to land.

Boots thudded against the wooden floors. Hats were tossed onto tables. Coats draped over chair backs. They were still dressed in their ranch clothing—fitted pants, sturdy boots, flowing shirts—but now their posture was different.

Heavy.

They had prayed before coming in.

Each woman bowed her head quietly at the door.

"Lord... help us not to harden our hearts," Magnolia whispered.

"Amen," they all said.

But prayer didn't erase feelings.

Then they all gathered in the parlor, the soft lamplight casting shadows across tired faces. This room smelled of lavender and old books—nothing like the jail, nothing like the courthouse.

Marisol dropped onto the sofa. "Well... I don't know about y'all... but I feel ambushed."

Millicent paced. "Cornered. That judge boxed us in."

Marigold crossed her arms. "Marriage or prison? That ain't no choice."

Margaret's voice shook. "I feel... ashamed."

Moonland leaned back in her chair. "I do too."

Silence fell.

Miyako finally spoke. "They embarrassed us."

Marisol scoffed. "They acted like we forced them."

Magnolia nodded. "Their attitude was clear."

She imitated Preston's tone, we didn't choose this.

"They acting like victims," Millicent said. "Like we dragged them to the altar."

Marigold slammed her hand on the table. "You can't make us love them, the men had said to the judge."

Everyone froze.

"That's the truth," Marigold continued. "Marriage don't mean heart."

Marisol nodded. "They wounded."

"Defensive," Moonland added. "Like cornered animals."

Miyako folded her hands. "They ashamed of how they living."

"And taking it out on us," Margaret whispered.

Millicent sighed. "They mad because we saw their mess."

Marisol snorted. "No chickens. No food. No curtains."

Marigold laughed. "House looked like a barn."

Magnolia raised a hand. "Ladies."

They quieted.

"We have to be careful," she said. "They hurting."

Marisol rolled her eyes. "So are we."

Magnolia nodded. "I know."

Moonland spoke softly. "Those men been alone too long."

"They don't know how to let women in," Margaret said.

"Rail life made them hard," Miyako added.

"Still," Marisol snapped, "that don't excuse their mouths."

Millicent smirked. "They called us bossy."

"Curvy," Marigold laughed. "Like it's an insult."

Marisol leaned forward. "They should thank God."

Laughter bubbled up.

Then it faded.

"They hurt us," Margaret whispered. "They made it sound like we're trouble."

Magnolia sighed. "They scared."

Magnolia stood. "Let's pray."

They joined hands.

"Father God…" Magnolia began. "We didn't ask for this."

"But you allowed it."

"Help us not to become bitter."

"Help us walk in wisdom."

"Help us not punish these men for our pain."

Marisol swallowed. "Lord… we mad."

Millicent added, "And hurt."

Marigold said, "And stubborn."

Moonland whispered, "But we yours."

Miyako said, "Teach us patience."

Margaret said, "Teach us love."

They all said, "Amen."

Venting

Prayer didn't stop them from venting.

Marisol flopped back on the sofa. "I swear if that man ever tells me to be quiet again…"

Millicent laughed. "I'll remind him who kissed who in court and them loving it."

Marigold shook her head. "They looked scared."

Margaret smiled faintly. "They did."

Moonland said, "They not used to women who fight back."

Miyako added, "Or think."

Marisol laughed. "Or cook."

They all laughed.

Magnolia smiled. "Alright... let's breathe."

Silence returned.

They stared into the fire.

Seven women.

Married.

To strangers.

Magnolia finally said quietly, "We don't have to love them today."

"But we will try to respect the covenant."

Marisol muttered, "Bare minimum."

They laughed again.

They sat together, still in boots, still in ranch clothes, processing what had just happened.

Their hearts were sore.

But they were not broken.

They were women who had survived worse.

And they would survive this too.

Millicent broke the silence first.

"We don't want men who feel forced upon us," she said, pacing slowly. "We want men who choose us."

Everyone nodded.

Magnolia lifted her chin. "We are beautifully and wonderfully made," she said softly. "The Bible says it."

Marisol snapped her fingers. "And they better start believing it."

Moonland leaned forward. "They our husbands now. Whether they like it or not."

Margaret added, "And Scripture says men ought to love their wives as Christ loved the church."

Miyako crossed her arms. "That means sacrifice."

"Respect," Marigold said.

"Protection," Millicent added.

Marisol shook her head. "But what did we get?"

"They rolled us in dirt," Marigold said.

"They grabbed us," Millicent added.

"They tried to tie us up," Marisol snapped.

Magnolia sighed. "And it ended in marriage... or jail."

"The pressure is on," Moonland said quietly.

They all sat with that truth.

Their Decision

Marisol stood. "I'm not living in no ragged ranch."

Millicent nodded. "We want the land split."

Magnolia looked around. "We build our own ranch."

Marigold smiled. "We grow our own produce."

"Raise our own chickens," Margaret added.

"Milk cows too," Millicent said.

Miyako added calmly, "We buy proper furniture."

Moonland nodded. "We do it right."

Marisol grinned. "And we got the money."

Marigold clapped. "We'll hire a full Mexican crew."

"Best builders," Millicent said.

"We put up tents on our portion of the land," Marisol added, "Oversee the work."

"Work all day," Moonland said.

"And stay here at night," Magnolia finished.

"The boardinghouse."

Silence.

Then smiles spread.

Millicent snapped her fingers. "After that..."

"We build our stores," Marisol said.

"Bakery," Margaret smiled.

"Sewing shop," Moonland said.

"Hair salon," Millicent added.

"Millinery," Marigold said.

Magnolia nodded. "We move forward."

Marisol crossed her arms. "They can stay mad."

Miyako said quietly, "We will stay focused."

Magnolia smiled softly. "God didn't bring us this far to fail."

They joined hands again.

"Lord... cover us," Magnolia prayed.

"Guide our steps."

"Help us walk in wisdom."

"Let our past not define our future."

"Let these marriages grow as they're meant to."

"And ... teach us how to still honor You."

"Amen."

They sat back.

97

Determined.

Calm.

Seven women who had faced worse storms.

This one...

They would navigate too.

When Power Came to Town

For the first time in his life, Preston Protect felt something unfamiliar settle in his chest.

Not fear.

Not anger.

Expectation.

Because power was coming to town.

And this time...

The women were ready.

The News Breaks

It started with a knock.

Not a polite knock. Not a soft one.

A commanding knock.

Sheriff Carter stood in the doorway of the boardinghouse parlor, hat in hand, face serious.

Magnolia rose first. "Yes, Sheriff?"

"They just posted it at the depot," he said. "Big meeting tomorrow."

"Who?" Millicent asked.

"A state senator. Cattle investors. Rail representatives."

Marisol straightened. "Power."

Sheriff nodded. "Money."

Moonland's eyes narrowed. "Influence."

Margaret whispered, "Decisions."

Miyako folded her arms. "They're here about land."

"Expansion," the sheriff confirmed. "Railroads. Grazing routes. Property rights."

Marigold laughed dryly. "So now they care."

Sheriff hesitated. "They'll be at the courthouse."

Silence.

Magnolia slowly smiled.

"Well," she said softly, "Looks like we dressed right for this town."

The Shift

They had lived around power before.

Washington, D.C. Velvet rooms. Men who whispered futures.

But this time...

They weren't behind curtains.

They weren't silent.

They were landowners. Businesswomen. Wives. Women of God.

Millicent's lips curved. "They don't know what's coming."

Marisol cracked her knuckles. "Not a clue."

Moonland breathed, "We didn't survive our past to be quiet now."

Margaret nodded. "We will be respectful... but firm."

Miyako added, "Strategic."

Marigold grinned. "Unforgettable."

Magnolia lifted her Bible from the side table. "We pray first."

They joined hands.

"Father God..." "You know power when it shows up." "You raise up and pull-down kings." "Give us wisdom." "Let our words cut through lies." "Cover us." "Go before us."

"Amen."

The Plan

They sat back down.

Millicent leaned forward. "We need to walk into that courthouse like we own it."

Marisol snapped. "We DO own it."

Moonland said quietly, "We speak truth."

"Control the room," Marigold added.

Magnolia nodded. "No emotion. Only clarity."

Miyako whispered, "They won't expect us."

Margaret smiled. "That's our advantage."

But First... The Homestead

Marisol stood abruptly. "Before tomorrow..."

"We go to the homestead," Millicent said.

Magnolia nodded. "Our land too."

Marigold laughed. "Time to place our demands."

Moonland stood. "Face to face."

They grabbed their hats.

Boots.

Gloves.

No fear.

Chapter Five

At the Ranch

The men were repairing a fence when they saw dust rise.

Seven figures approached.

Walking.

Not wagons.

Not shy.

Preston squinted. "Lord…"

Parker muttered, "Here they come."

Paxton whispered, "Jesus help us."

They stopped working.

The women marched straight up.

Not angry.

Resolved.

Magnolia spoke first.

"We own this land too."

Silence.

Preston nodded slowly. "We know."

Millicent crossed her arms. "We're not here to fight."

Parker exhaled. "Praise God."

Marisol added, "We're here to set terms."

Phoenix stiffened. "Terms?"

Moonland said calmly, "We want the land split."

Porter blinked. "Half?"

"Yes," Margaret said.

Miyako added, "We will build our own ranch."

Marigold smiled. "With good wood."

Millicent continued, "We'll grow produce."

"Raise chickens."

"Milk cows."

"Buy furniture."

Marisol smirked. "We not living like cavemen."

Paxton muttered, "That hurt."

Magnolia raised her hand. "You keep your house."

"We build ours."

Pierce frowned. "Y'all serious?"

Moonland replied, "Very."

Marisol added, "We'll hire builders."

"Full Mexican crew," Marigold said. "Fast. Professional."

Pablo raised his eyebrows. "They good."

Magnolia continued, "We'll put up tents."

"Oversee the work."

"Stay at the boardinghouse at night."

Preston swallowed. "You don't need us."

Millicent replied, "No."

Silence hit hard.

The Men React

Parker scratched his beard. "So y'all moving out."

Margaret said softly, "Yes."

Paxton frowned. "We married and we figured we live together."

Marisol snapped, "Doesn't mean we move in, you just want women to sleep with."

Phoenix crossed his arms. "You don't trust us."

Moonland answered, "Not yet."

Porter sighed. "That hurts."

Magnolia met his eyes. "So did the dirt."

Silence.

Then Preston stepped forward.

"Fair."

Everyone looked at him.

"You got money." "You got vision." "We been surviving."

He nodded. "You deserve better."

106

The men exchanged glances.

Pierce muttered, "We need to step up."

Paxton nodded. "Truth."

Setting Boundaries

Magnolia spoke clearly.

"We don't want men who feel forced and just want our bodies."

"We want men who choose us."

Marisol added, "We beautifully and wonderfully made."

Millicent snapped, "Bible says it."

Moonland continued, "Scripture says husbands love wives like Christ loved the church."

Marigold smirked. "You got some growing to do."

Miyako added, "And so do we."

Preston nodded. "We'll respect your plan."

Porter said quietly, "You free to build."

Pablo swallowed. "We ain't stopping you."

Phoenix looked down. "We'll earn it."

A Shift

For the first time...

No shouting.

No insults.

Just truth.

Magnolia softened. "We're not enemies."

Marisol sighed. "We just won't be controlled."

Paxton whispered, "Understood."

Millicent turned back to them.

"By the way..."

"Big meeting tomorrow."

"Senator."

"Cattle investors."

"Rail men."

The men stiffened.

Preston muttered, "That's big."

Magnolia smiled.

"We'll be there."

The men looked shocked.

"In the courthouse," Marisol added.

Moonland said calmly, "Front row."

Miyako whispered, "They won't expect us."

Marigold grinned. "But they will remember us."

They Leave

They turned.

Walked back down the dusty path.

Seven women.

United.

Strong.

Not angry.

Purposeful.

The men stood frozen.

Parker finally said, "We married power."

Paxton laughed nervously. "We married hurricanes."

Preston whispered, "Or destiny."

From the boardinghouse window, Magnolia looked out over the town.

"Power is coming," she whispered.

Millicent smiled. "And this time..."

Marisol snapped, "We ready."

Moonland breathed, "For the first time..."

Margaret finished, "In our lives."

Miyako said, "We won't hide."

Marigold grinned, "Let's go change something."

"Father God…" "You raise leaders and remove them." "Give us wisdom." "Let our words pierce pride." "Cover us." "Go before us."

"Amen."

Millicent nodded. "We're still not moving in."

Magnolia agreed. "Marriage don't mean access."

Moonland added, "They need to earn trust."

Margaret whispered, "Respect."

Miyako said calmly, "Growth."

Marigold grinned. "We still running our own lives."

They all agreed.

At the Homestead (They Visit — Not Stay)

They did not move in. They did not unpack. They did not soften.

Chapter Six - Courthouse

Inside the courthouse, the energy shifted.

Not curiosity. Recognition.

Not flirtation. Attention.

They moved as one unit.

No rushing. No hesitation.

Marisol whispered, "They watching."

Millicent murmured, "Good."

Men Notice

Across the room, their husbands stood near the back.

Paxton froze. "Lord..."

Parker swallowed. "Different women."

Phoenix whispered, "They look..."

Porter finished, "Powerful."

Pierce said nothing. Just stared.

Preston's chest tightened. "They ain't playing."

Paxton muttered, "I forgot they used to move with senators."

Parker nodded. "They in their element."

A cattle investor leaned to Preston.

"Who are they?"

Preston hesitated. "Our... wives."

The man blinked. "All seven?"

Preston exhaled. "Yes."

The investor looked impressed. "You married well."

Preston didn't answer.

Inside Their Circle

Marisol whispered, "See how they look at us?"

Millicent smiled. "They see authority."

Moonland added, "They don't know why."

Magnolia replied, "They don't need to."

Miyako's eyes scanned the room. "We speak when it's time."

Marigold cracked her knuckles discreetly. "Ready."

A senator's aide approached. "Ladies, may I help you?"

Magnolia smiled. "We're here to listen."

"Landowners," Millicent added.

The aide nodded slowly. "Front row."

They moved forward.

No argument.

No hesitation.

They sat.

Silence followed.

Their Husbands Watching

Paxton whispered, "They different."

Parker nodded. "They not mad."

Phoenix said quietly, "They strategic."

Porter muttered, "We been underestimating them."

Pierce crossed his arms. "Badly."

Preston's eyes stayed on Magnolia. "She ain't here for us."

Pablo said softly, "She here for something bigger."

Magnolia folded her gloves neatly.

"Power thinks it owns rooms," she whispered.

Millicent smiled. "But presence does."

Marisol breathed, "Let's change the air."

Moonland added, "In Jesus' name."

Miyako nodded. "Amen."

Marigold grinned. "Game time."

Their Pitch

The room quieted when Magnolia stood.

Not because she demanded attention. Because her presence commanded it.

She didn't rush. She didn't smile. She simply placed her gloved hands on the table in front of her and looked straight at the senator.

"We are landowners," Magnolia said calmly.

Her voice carried. Not loud. Certain.

Millicent stepped beside her.

"We are building businesses," she added. "Permanent businesses. Not fly-by-night operations."

Marisol leaned in, eyes steady.

"We lease to women leaving the life."

A murmur rippled across the room.

Moonland spoke next, her tone soft but piercing.

"Women escaping prostitution. Abuse. Exploitation."

Margaret continued.

"We provide housing. Skills training. Dignity."

Miyako folded her hands.

"Tailoring. Baking. Hair care. Hat making."

Marigold finished.

"Work that feeds families."

Silence dropped like a curtain.

Magnolia lifted her chin.

"We are reducing crime."

Millicent added.

"Reducing poverty."

Marisol said slowly.

"And restoring women who society threw away."

The room shifted.

This wasn't emotion. This was strategy.

Economics.

Morality.

Politics.

All wrapped in one clean message.

The senator leaned back slowly.

Eyes sharp.

Listening.

The Senator's Interest

Senator Edgar Whitmore finally spoke.

"How many jobs?" he asked.

Millicent answered instantly.

"Forty within six months. Eighty by next year."

He blinked.

Magnolia added.

"Women. Men. Apprentices."

"How much land?" he asked.

Moonland replied.

"160 acres homestead. Additional town lots."

"Who funds you?" he pressed.

Marisol smiled.

"We do."

The room gasped.

"Our own capital," Margaret said.

"No government money."

"No charity."

"Investment," Miyako said.

"Profit with purpose," Marigold added.

The senator's pen froze.

"You are… self-funded?"

Magnolia nodded.

"We earned it."

He studied them.

Not their clothes.

Not their curves.

Their discipline.

"And what do you want from the state?" he asked.

Millicent replied.

"Zoning approval."

"Protection from predatory investors," Marisol added.

"Access to rail shipment," Moonland said.

"Fair contracts," Margaret finished.

Silence again.

Men's Reaction

Their husbands stood frozen.

Paxton whispered.

"They planned this."

Parker swallowed.

"They dangerous."

Phoenix shook his head.

"They not playing games."

Porter muttered.

"They sound like lawyers."

Pierce stared.

"I didn't know my wife could talk like that."

Preston felt his chest tighten.

I married a general.

Cattlemen Reaction

One cattle baron snorted.

"Women in business?" he scoffed.

"They'll be crying in six months."

Another leaned back.

"Land ain't for emotions."

Marisol turned slowly.

"Neither is hunger."

The room stilled.

Millicent added.

"Or crime."

Moonland said calmly.

"Or broken homes."

A younger rancher nodded.

"They smart."

An older man rubbed his chin.

"Profit with purpose... that's new."

Another said.

"Rail will back this."

Conflict brewed.

Sneers.

Nods.

Whispers.

Power shifting.

The Senator Smiles

Senator Whitmore finally smiled.

Slow.

Measured.

"I didn't expect this today."

Magnolia replied.

"Neither did we."

"But God did," Marigold muttered.

The senator stood.

"Ladies... I want a private meeting."

Gasps.

He pointed.

"Tonight."

The Husbands

Paxton grabbed Parker's arm.

"They just changed everything."

Phoenix whispered.

"We underestimated them."

Preston swallowed hard.

"I did."

As the women gathered their gloves, Magnolia whispered.

"See?"

Millicent smiled.

"Power listens."

Marisol snapped.

"When you speak its language."

Moonland added.

"Truth."

Margaret said.

"Preparation."

Miyako whispered.

"Purpose."

Marigold grinned.

"Let's go shake something else."

They walked out.

Heads high.

Seven husbands watched in awe.

For the first time...

They weren't embarrassed.

They were proud.

Chapter Seven

When Power Starts to Bend**

The room didn't return to normal after the women finished speaking.

It couldn't.

Something had shifted in the courthouse air. Not noise. Not chaos. Authority. The kind that didn't need to shout.

The cattlemen in the back shuffled in their seats. Boots scraped wood. Hats tilted lower. Whispers began to ripple.

One older rancher snorted. "Women in business?" he muttered to his neighbor. "That won't last."

His neighbor, a younger man with sunburned skin and tired eyes, leaned back. "Don't know about that. They got their numbers straight."

Another cattle baron, thick mustached, scoffed. "They soft. This land eats soft people alive."

Marisol turned slightly in her seat and looked straight at him.

"Sir," she said calmly, "soft people don't survive what we survived."

Silence.

Millicent added, "And they don't build businesses."

Moonland said quietly, "They hide."

The rancher swallowed and looked away.

Across the aisle, a cattle investor whispered, "Smart investment."

His friend nodded. "They self-funded. That's rare."

"Forty jobs in six months," another murmured. "That's real money."

A gray-haired man rubbed his chin. "They thinking long-term."

Conflict bubbled.

Sneers. Nods. Power negotiating itself in real time.

The Private Meetings Begin

As soon as the session paused, men began circling.

Not shouting. Approaching.

A tall cattleman with a silver belt buckle stepped forward first.

"My name's Thomas Crowley," he said. "I own land east of town."

Magnolia shook his hand. "Pleasure."

He lowered his voice. "I respect what you're doing."

Marigold raised an eyebrow. "Do you?"

"Yes, ma'am," he said. "My sister ran from that life. Never made it out."

The women softened.

"If you need pasture lease later," he said, "I'm open."

Millicent smiled. "We'll remember that."

Then a banker appeared. Clean suit. Polished shoes.

"Gentlemen, ladies," he said. "Nathaniel Porter, First Territorial Bank."

Porter Protect stiffened. "Another Porter."

The banker laughed. "No relation."

He turned to Magnolia. "You said self-funded?"

"Yes."

"I'd like to discuss interest options," he said. "Expansion loans. You're low risk."

Margaret blinked. "They calling us low risk."

Miyako whispered, "We prepared."

The banker handed a card. "Private meeting?"

Magnolia nodded. "Soon."

Then the senator approached.

Edgar Whitmore.

He held out his card.

"I want to continue this conversation," he said. "Tonight."

Gasps rippled.

Millicent smiled. "We'll come."

Momentum.

Pure momentum.

The Recognition

A man stepped forward slowly.

He was dressed well. Gold watch. Sharp eyes.

"I knew you once," he said.

The room stilled.

Everyone turned.

Marisol's body went rigid.

She faced him slowly.

"You knew who I was," she said evenly.

His lips twitched. "Back in D.C."

Her eyes locked on his.

"You knew my past," she said. "But you don't know me now."

The room went silent.

Her voice didn't shake.

"I don't live there anymore."

"I don't belong to that world."

"I belong to God."

"I belong to my purpose."

She leaned in slightly.

"You knew who I was."

Then she stepped back.

"You know me now."

The man flushed.

Whispers exploded.

The husbands froze.

Paxton whispered, "She just buried him alive."

Parker murmured, "Clean."

Phoenix exhaled. "She powerful."

The Power Scene Expands

Another man whispered, "That woman used to—"

Another man cut him off. "She used to survive. Mind your mouth."

More murmurs.

The senator watched carefully.

He wasn't laughing now.

He was calculating.

By evening, news traveled.

The newspaper editor burst into the courthouse.

"Ladies," he said breathless. "I want your story."

Magnolia nodded. "Tomorrow."

By sunset:

A senator drafted a letter of support • A banker opened credit talks • Three donors pledged seed money • A cattleman offered land lease • Town whispers turned to respect

The headline was already forming:

SEVEN WOMEN SHAKE REDSTONE

The husbands stood back.

Watching.

Absorbing.

Paxton whispered, "They changing history."

Parker nodded. "I married a storm."

Preston swallowed.

"I married a leader."

The Romance Angle

Later, outside, the men gathered.

Not boasting. Not joking.

Reflecting.

Phoenix said quietly, "She ain't scared."

Pierce nodded. "She dangerous."

Porter Protect whispered, "I never seen my wife command a room like that."

Pablo shook his head. "She didn't even raise her voice."

Paxton laughed softly. "I thought I was tough."

Parker looked at Millicent through the window. "She different."

Preston stared at Magnolia.

"She's built for this."

Silence.

Then Parker said, "Proud of y'all?"

Preston nodded.

"Terrified too."

They laughed.

The Twist

Late that night, Senator Whitmore met privately with his aide.

"They impressive," the aide said.

The senator nodded. "Too impressive."

"You don't trust them?"

He sighed.

"I oppose women owning land."

The aide blinked.

"Sir?"

"I support the railroad."

"Major investors back me."

"Those women threaten land consolidation."

The aide frowned. "But you smiled."

"I play chess," Whitmore said. "Not checkers."

He poured whiskey.

"They don't know I have rail ties."

"So what now?" the aide asked.

He smiled slowly.

"I let them think I support them."

"Then I move quietly."

The aide swallowed.

"You going to undermine them?"

The senator leaned back.

"Power never gives space willingly."
134

From the boardinghouse window, Magnolia watched the town lights.

Millicent stood beside her. "You feel it?"

"Yes," Magnolia said. "Resistance."

Marisol laughed. "Good."

Moonland whispered, "We prayed for this."

Margaret smiled. "We ready."

Miyako said, "Whatever comes."

Marigold grinned. "Let's go to war."

The men stood outside the boardinghouse.

Watching.

Not with fear.

With reverence.

Because they didn't just marry women.

They married destiny.

When Power Shows Its Teeth

The first sign of betrayal did not come with shouting.

It came with paper.

A neatly folded document slid across Senator Whitmore's desk as he sat in his hotel suite, staring out at the lamplit street of Redstone. His aide, a thin man named Granger, waited silently.

"The rail consortium sent it," Granger said. "Terms."

Whitmore unfolded it slowly.

Land acquisition. Eminent domain. Expansion routes.

Right through the women's homestead.

Whitmore's jaw tightened.

"They want it all," he muttered. "Every acre."

Granger nodded. "They say women-owned land complicates negotiations."

Whitmore leaned back. "Of course they do."

He tapped the paper.

"They funded my last campaign."

"So?" Granger asked.

"So..." Whitmore said quietly, "Power doesn't argue. It absorbs."

He stood.

"Those women are a threat."

"Not because they're loud," he added. "But because they're effective."

Granger hesitated. "You told them you supported them."

Whitmore smiled thinly.

"I told them what they needed to hear."

Rail Company Moves

The next morning, wagons rolled in.

Not farm wagons.

Survey wagons.

Men in suits stepped off trains. Maps. Measuring rods. Stakes.

Redstone buzzed.

"They marking land," someone whispered.

"The railroad," another said.

At the boardinghouse, Magnolia read the notice posted on the door.

Her face hardened.

"They filing for expansion rights."

Millicent snatched the paper. "Through our land."

Marisol's voice dropped. "They lying."

Moonland whispered, "They smiling too much."

Margaret swallowed. "They using law."

Miyako read quietly. "Eminent domain."

Marigold slammed her hand on the table. "So they stealing."

Magnolia looked up. "This is why power smiled."

Silence fell.

The Senator's Public Face

That afternoon, Whitmore held a public meeting.

Same smile. Same charm.

"The railroad brings progress," he said. "Jobs."

"We must sacrifice for growth."

Magnolia stood.

"You promised to protect landowners."

Whitmore spread his hands. "I still will."

"But some progress requires compromise."

Millicent stepped forward. "Not theft."

Whitmore's smile tightened.

"Ladies," he said, "Be reasonable."

Marisol snapped. "We earned that land."

Whitmore nodded. "And now the state needs it."

Moonland said softly, "You betrayed us."

Gasps rippled.

139

Whitmore's eyes hardened.

"You don't understand politics."

Magnolia replied, "We understand character."

Women Counter-Strategy

That night, the boardinghouse parlor became war room.

Maps spread. Papers stacked.

Magnolia spoke first.

"We fight smart."

Millicent nodded. "Legally."

Marisol said, "Publicly."

Moonland added, "Spiritually."

Margaret whispered, "Strategically."

Miyako tapped the map. "They need public support."

Marigold grinned. "Let's give it to them."

Step One – The Press

Magnolia walked into the newspaper office.

"You want a story?" she asked.

Editor's eyes lit. "Always."

"Railroad stealing women's land."

The pen scratched.

Step Two – The Church

Moonland spoke at the revival service.

"Justice isn't gendered," she said. "God defends the widow."

Amen thundered.

Step Three – The Donors

Millicent met with Crowley, the banker.

"They breaking contracts," she said.

Crowley's jaw tightened. "Not on my watch."

Step Four – Legal Action

Margaret filed injunctions.

"Paper beats paper," she said quietly.

Step Five – Community

Marigold went door to door.

"Would you let them take your land?"

People shook heads.

The Men Watch

At the ranch, the husbands argued.

Paxton paced. "They coming for our land too."

Parker said, "We should ride into town."

Phoenix shook his head. "They told us not to interfere."

Porter muttered, "They don't need saving."

Pierce added, "They saving themselves."

Preston stared at the horizon.

"They right."

First Cracks in the Marriages

That night, Preston went to the boardinghouse.

Magnolia opened the door.

"We asked for space," she said.

"I know," he replied. "But they taking our land."

"Our land," she corrected.

He flinched.

"That's what I mean," he said.

Silence.

"You don't trust me," he added.

Magnolia folded her arms. "You dragged me through mud."

He swallowed.

"And you kissed me in front of a courtroom," he said.

Her eyes softened.

"That was survival," she whispered.

"I don't know how to be your husband," he admitted.

She said quietly, "Then learn."

Door closed.

Paxton and Marigold

Paxton found Marigold on the boardwalk that evening.

"You hate me?"

She laughed bitterly. "I don't know you."

"That hurt."

"So did the rope," she snapped.

Silence.

"Help us fight," he said.

She studied him. "Show me."

Millicent and Parker

Parker brought flowers.

She stared.

"What is this?"

"I don't know," he said. "Trying."

She took them slowly.

"Don't quit," she said.

Loyalty Tested

Rail men came to the ranch and offered bribes.

To the husbands.

"Walk away," they said. "Sell."

Paxton slammed the door.

Pierce punched the wall.

Phoenix spat. "Never."

Preston rode straight to Magnolia.

"They offered money."

She froze.

"And?"

"I told them no."

Her eyes searched his.

"You choosing me?"

"I'm choosing what's right."

The Senator's Counter-Move

Whitmore watched the town shift.

Support growing.

Petitions.

Church sermons.

He slammed his desk.

"They outmaneuvering me."

Granger swallowed. "Sir... they strong."

Whitmore sneered. "They still women."

Granger hesitated.

"They don't act like it."

The Public Clash

At the depot, Magnolia confronted Whitmore.

"You lied."

He smiled thin. "You misunderstand."

"No," she said. "You underestimated."

Crowd gathered.

Millicent added, "We have contracts."

Margaret held papers. "Injunction filed."

Whitmore stiffened.

"You'll regret this."

Marisol laughed. "Already survived worse men than you."

Cheers erupted.

Closing

That night, Magnolia prayed.

"Lord... we didn't ask for war."

"But we won't run."

Across town, Preston prayed too.

"Make me a man worthy."

Power clashed.

Politics burned.

Love trembled.

But loyalty...

Loyalty was chosen.

Chapter Seven

The courthouse steps were crowded before sunrise.

Men in suits. Farmers in boots. Women clutching baskets. Children perched on fences.

Word had traveled fast.

The railroad was being challenged. And seven women were standing in the middle of it.

Magnolia stood at the top of the steps, gloves folded neatly in her hand. Her posture was straight, unshaken. Beside her stood Millicent, Marisol, Moonland, Margaret, Miyako, and Marigold — each one steady, eyes forward.

Behind them, their husbands hovered.

Not in front. Not controlling.

Watching.

Learning.

The Injunction Hearing

Judge Whitmore entered the chamber.

The same judge who married them.

His eyes lingered on them for a moment — thoughtful.

"Court is now in session."

The railroad attorney stood.

Gray suit. Cold smile.

"Your honor," he began, "the railroad expansion is a matter of state progress."

Magnolia rose.

"With all respect," she said, "progress that steals land is theft."

Gasps.

The attorney smirked. "Madam, you are emotional."

Millicent stepped forward.

"No," she said calmly. "We are prepared."

Margaret held up documents.

"Injunction filed."

Miyako continued.

"Fraudulent survey boundaries."

Moonland added.

"Conflict of interest."

Marigold finished.

"Bribery."

The courtroom erupted.

Judge Whitmore slammed his gavel.

"ORDER."

The attorney froze.

"You have evidence?" the judge asked.

Magnolia nodded.

"Signed contracts."

"Campaign donations."

"Witnesses."

She handed papers to the clerk.

Judge Whitmore adjusted his glasses.

He read.

Silence thickened.

The Senator Exposed

Senator Whitmore shifted in his seat.

His face tightened.

The judge looked up.

"Senator," he said slowly, "care to explain why rail funds appear in your personal accounts?"

Whitmore stood.

"Campaign support," he said stiffly.

"For land seizure?" the judge pressed.

Whitmore faltered.

Magnolia's voice cut through.

"You told us you supported women-owned land."

Whitmore snapped.

"Politics change."

Marisol leaned forward.

"So does integrity?"

Crowd murmured.

Judge Whitmore banged the gavel.

"Senator Edgar Whitmore, you are now being investigated."

Whitmore's face drained.

The Husbands Step Forward

Preston moved.

He stood beside Magnolia.

"My wife speaks truth."

Phoenix followed.

"So does mine."

One by one, the men stepped forward.

No hesitation.

No fear.

Paxton cleared his throat.

"They tried to bribe us."

Gasps.

Parker added.

"We said no."

Porter spoke.

"They offered money to walk away."

Judge Whitmore's eyes narrowed.

"You will give statements."

They nodded.

First Real Marriage Moment

Magnolia glanced at Preston.

"You chose us."

He met her gaze.

"Today... yes."

Her eyes softened.

Not forgiveness.

But respect.

Public Reaction

The newspaper editor scribbled furiously.

"TITAN FALLS," he muttered.

Women in the crowd whispered.

"They standing up."

Men nodded.

"About time."

A farmer shouted.

"Leave our land alone!"

Cheers erupted.

The Railroad Retreats

The attorney gathered his papers.

"This hearing is premature."

Judge Whitmore cut him off.

"No."

"Injunction granted."

"Railroad expansion HALTED pending investigation."

The room exploded.

Applause.

Cries.

Whistles.

Magnolia closed her eyes.

Thank You, Lord.

After Court

Outside, reporters swarmed.

"Mrs. Brownland!" "What's next?"

She answered calmly.

"We build."

Millicent added.

"We hire."

Marisol smirked.

"We rise."

Private Moment

Later, Preston found Magnolia alone.

"I was wrong," he said.

She didn't answer.

"You didn't deserve how we treated you."

Silence.

He whispered.

"I want to learn."

She finally spoke.

"Learning starts with listening."

He nodded.

"I'm listening."

The Senator's Fall

That evening, telegrams flew.

Whitmore under investigation. Rail ties exposed. Donors pulling out.

Granger packed his bags.

"You're finished," he muttered.

Whitmore stared at the wall.

"They beat me."

Spiritual Undercurrent

That night, the women gathered again.

Hands joined.

"Thank you, Lord."

Moonland whispered.

"You fought for us."

Margaret added.

"You defended our land."

Miyako smiled.

"We give You glory."

Marigold laughed.

"And we still building."

The men stood outside.

Preston whispered.

"I married a leader."

Phoenix nodded.

"Me too."

Paxton said.

"And I almost messed it up."

Parker smiled.

"But you didn't."

Magnolia opened her Bible.

"Isaiah 54," she read.

"No weapon formed against you shall prosper."

They all said amen.

The Calling Card

They didn't celebrate long.

Victory in court didn't mean the war was over.

Magnolia closed the courthouse doors behind them and exhaled slowly. "We're not finished."

Millicent nodded. "He still breathing."

Marisol's eyes narrowed. "And we know his past."

Moonland said quietly, "All of it."

Margaret swallowed. "He knew us."

Miyako added, "Before."

Marigold smirked. "When he thought we were disposable."

They stood in a tight circle.

Seven women. One shared history. One final card to play.

Magnolia spoke carefully. "We don't threaten lightly."

Millicent added, "But we won't be bullied."

Marisol crossed her arms. "We use wisdom."

Moonland nodded. "And truth."

They all agreed.

The Invitation

A note was delivered that afternoon.

Handwritten.

Firm.

"Senator Whitmore, We request a private meeting this evening at the boardinghouse parlor. You owe us that much."

He read it twice.

His jaw tightened.

Evening – Boardinghouse Parlor

Oil lamps glowed soft gold. The parlor was quiet. No gossip. No crowd. Just silence and history.

Whitmore arrived alone.

No aide.

No bravado.

The women waited seated.

Not aggressive.

Not afraid.

Magnolia gestured to a chair. "Sit."

He did.

"You called?" he said stiffly.

Marisol smiled faintly. "You know why."

His eyes moved over their faces.

Recognition flickered.

"You look... different."

Millicent replied, "We are."

Moonland said softly, "But you knew us."

He shifted.

"In Washington."

Margaret's voice was calm. "When you and your friends came through."

Miyako added, "When we were hostesses."

He swallowed.

Marigold leaned forward. "When you thought we were invisible."

Silence pressed heavy.

They Speak Their Truth

Magnolia stood.

"We gave our hearts to God."

"We left that life."

"We changed."

Millicent continued, "You should have too."

Marisol's voice sharpened. "But instead you built power on broken backs."

Moonland said quietly, "Women like us."

Whitmore clenched his fists.

"You think I'm proud of it?"

Margaret replied, "Pride isn't the issue."

"Accountability is," Miyako said.

The Leverage

Magnolia's voice dropped.

"We know things about you."

Whitmore stiffened.

"Details," Marisol added. "Names."

"Dates," Millicent said.

"Deals," Moonland whispered.

"Women," Margaret finished.

Miyako leaned forward. "Men in your circle."

Marigold smiled coldly. "Enough to end careers."

Whitmore snapped, "If you expose me, you expose yourselves."

Silence.

Then Magnolia said softly, "No."

"You expose a system."

Millicent added, "You lift other women."

Marisol leaned closer. "You show them they're not alone."

Moonland said, "That powerful men don't get to erase them."

Margaret whispered, "That God redeems."

Miyako nodded. "And justice speaks."

Whitmore's face drained.

"You'd destroy your reputation."

Marigold laughed. "Our reputation was built by men like you."

"You can't break what we already rebuilt."

The Ultimatum

Magnolia straightened.

"You have a choice."

"Tomorrow," Millicent said, "You drop the suit."

Marisol added, "Publicly."

Moonland continued, "No more rail interference."

Margaret said, "Or..."

Miyako finished, "We go public."

Marigold smiled. "With names."

Whitmore stood abruptly.

"You're blackmailing me."

Magnolia shook her head.

"No."

"We're holding you accountable."

"Your choice determines the ending."

The Weight of It

Whitmore paced.

"You don't understand the pressure."

Marisol snapped, "You don't understand survival."

Moonland said quietly, "You used us."

"Now choose."

He stopped pacing.

Looked at each face.

Not women he once controlled.

But women he now feared.

"You'd really do it?" he whispered.

Magnolia met his eyes.

"Yes."

The Departure

He picked up his coat slowly.

"I'll think about it."

Millicent replied, "Think fast."

Marisol added, "Court's in the morning."

Whitmore nodded once.

Then left.

The door closed.

Aftermath

Silence.

Margaret exhaled. "That was heavy."

Moonland said, "But necessary."

Miyako whispered, "Truth always costs."

Marigold laughed softly. "Worth it."

Magnolia sat.

"We didn't threaten him."

Millicent smiled. "We gave him a choice."

Marisol leaned back. "Power hates choices."

They joined hands.

"Lord... we leave this in Your hands."

"Amen."

The Senator's Decision

The courthouse was standing-room only.

Word had spread like wildfire through Redstone. Farmers. Shopkeepers. Church women. Rail men. Investors. Everyone wanted to see what would happen next.

Judge Whitmore took his seat.

"Court is now in session."

A hush fell.

Senator Edgar Whitmore entered slowly.

No confident stride. No political smile. Just measured steps.

People leaned forward.

The railroad attorney whispered urgently. "Senator, we have leverage."

Whitmore lifted a hand. "No."

The attorney froze.

Judge Whitmore raised an eyebrow. "Senator Whitmore, you have the floor."

Whitmore stood.

Cleared his throat.

"Your Honor," he began, "after careful consideration... I am withdrawing my support from the railroad expansion through the disputed lands."

Gasps erupted.

"What?" "He's backing out?" "No way!"

The attorney turned pale. "You can't—"

Whitmore cut him off.

"I can."

He faced the room.

"This court, this town, these landowners deserve fairness."

Magnolia sat motionless.

Millicent's fingers tightened on her gloves.

Marisol whispered, "He chose right."

Moonland breathed, "Thank You, God."

Whitmore continued.

"I formally request dismissal of the suit."

Silence.

Then Judge Whitmore spoke.

"Request granted."

The gavel struck.

BANG.

Pandemonium.

Public Retreat

Whitmore stepped back.

Reporters surged.

"Senator!" "Why the reversal?" "Political pressure?"

He adjusted his coat.

"I listened."

That was all he said.

He left through a side door.

No speeches. No excuses. Just retreat.

Town Shock

Outside, voices exploded.

"Did you hear that?" "He dropped it!" "Those women scared him!"

A farmer laughed. "Good!"

A shopkeeper said, "Power met power."

Church women hugged.

"They did it!"

Children cheered.

Newspaper Fallout

By afternoon, the headlines screamed:

SENATOR RETREATS — SEVEN WOMEN WIN LAND WAR

RAIL EXPANSION HALTED — WOMEN-LED BUSINESSES RISE

REDEMPTION & RESOLVE — FROM SHADOWS TO STRENGTH

Photographs splashed the front page.

The women standing tall. Hats tilted. Eyes forward.

The article read:

"These women, once known only in whispers, now stand as pillars of economic and moral reform in Redstone..."

Donors began arriving.

Letters poured in.

Church groups pledged support.

Businessmen requested meetings.

The Husbands Watching

In the back of the courtroom, the seven men remained.

Not moving.

Not speaking.

Just watching.

Paxton whispered, "We married giants."

Parker shook his head. "I thought I was tough."

Phoenix muttered, "They don't flinch."

Porter said quietly, "They stared down a senator."

Pierce exhaled. "I don't know her."

Preston's eyes stayed locked on Magnolia.

"I married a leader."

But they were husbands in name only.

No shared home. No shared bed. No shared routine.

But something shifted.

Respect.

Reverence.

A quiet fear of the women they thought they knew.

Private Realization

Paxton murmured, "We got to step up."

Parker nodded. "They ain't waiting on us."

Phoenix added, "They don't need saving."

Porter whispered, "They building empires."

Preston swallowed hard.

"And I don't want to be the man who stands in her way."

Magnolia stood as reporters swarmed.

"Mrs. Brownland!" "How does it feel?"

She answered calmly.

"Justice feels right."

Millicent added, "Power listens when truth speaks."

Marisol smiled. "And we not done."

Moonland said softly, "This is only the beginning."

Margaret nodded. "For this town."

Miyako whispered, "For women."

Marigold grinned. "For God."

They walked out together.

Not looking back.

Seven women.

Victorious.

Seven men followed.

Husbands by law.

Students by choice.

Boots on the Ground

The next morning, the women did not wake up as celebrities.

They woke up as builders.

The newspaper lay folded on the parlor table, bold headlines screaming their victory, but none of them touched it. Fame was loud. Work was louder.

They dressed in their ranch clothing.

Tightly fitted pants that allowed movement. Billowing shirts that caught the wind. Wide leather belts. Riding boots scuffed from purpose. Hats pulled low.

They looked like ranchers.

Not society women. Not courtroom warriors.

Workers.

Marisol adjusted her hat in the mirror. "Today we build."

Millicent tied her gloves tight. "No speeches."

Moonland nodded. "Only action."

Magnolia grabbed the blueprint. "Tents first."

Construction Begins

Wagons rolled up the road.

Canvas. Lumber. Tool chests.

The Mexican crew arrived early—strong men, laughing, ready to work.

Magnolia greeted the foreman.

"Señor Alvarez."

"Buenos días, señora," he smiled.

"We start today."

He nodded. "Fast work."

The women spread out the land map.

Miyako pointed. "Tents here."

Margaret added, "Kitchen tent downwind."

Marigold laughed. "Sleeping tents away from snoring."

Millicent snapped, "Let's move."

Hammers rang.

Canvas stretched.

Ropes tightened.

Poles lifted.

Dust rose.

They worked beside the crew.

No hesitation.

No fear.

The Men Appear

Seven horses appeared at the ridge.

The husbands.

They slowed.

Watched.

Preston squinted. "They already started."

Paxton muttered. "They didn't wait."

Parker cleared his throat. "Should we... help?"

Phoenix said quietly, "They didn't ask."

They rode closer.

Stopped.

Preston dismounted.

Magnolia saw him.

Looked away.

Millicent whispered, "Ignore."

They kept working.

Preston approached.

"Y'all need help?"

Silence.

Marisol lifted a beam without looking at him.

Paxton tried again. "We can lift."

Moonland tied a rope.

No response.

Porter swallowed. "They ignoring us."

Pierce muttered, "Deserved."

The crew worked around them.

Magnolia finally spoke.

"We're fine."

Cold. Final.

Awkward First Teamwork

Paxton grabbed a post anyway.

Marigold snapped. "Put it down."

He froze.

"We got men working," she said. "They were hired."

Phoenix said softly, "We just want to help."

Moonland turned.

"Help is chosen," she said. "Not forced."

Silence.

Parker rubbed his neck. "We married."

Millicent laughed without humor. "By threat."

Marisol finally faced Pablo.

"You didn't choose me."

"You chose not to go to jail."

He flinched.

"That different."

The men stepped back.

Rejected.

Why They Refuse

Magnolia walked up to Preston.

"We don't want men who feel obligated."

"We want men who want us."

"Who choose us."

"Not husbands by court order."

Preston swallowed.

"That hurt."

"Truth does," she replied.

Marisol added, "We survived men who pretended."

Moonland said quietly, "We won't repeat it."

Margaret whispered, "We gave our hearts to God."

"Not to pressure."

Miyako added, "We are building without you."

"For now."

Emotional Breakthroughs

The men stood aside.

Watching.

Sweat on women's brows.

Laughter.

Strength.

Paxton whispered, "They don't need us."

Parker shook his head. "They don't trust us."

Phoenix said softly, "Yet."

Preston stared at Magnolia.

"She serious."

Pierce swallowed. "So am I."

They mounted their horses.

Not angry.

Reflective.

Later That Evening

The tents stood tall.

Canvas snapping in wind.

Cooking fires started.

The women sat together.

Exhausted.

Satisfied.

Marisol laughed. "We did that."

Millicent smiled. "They didn't touch one nail."

Moonland said softly, "That felt good."

Magnolia exhaled.

"We building on our own terms."

The Men Watching from Afar

From the ridge, the men watched the lanterns glow.

Paxton whispered, "They didn't look back."

Parker said, "They strong."

Phoenix nodded. "We need to earn."

Preston clenched his jaw.

"I will."

Closing Beat

Magnolia stared at the stars.

"Lord," she whispered, "we walk forward."

"Not backward."

Millicent added, "Not settling."

Marisol smiled. "For the first time... we choose."

Moonland breathed. "And we wait to be chosen."

Faith Without Works Is Dead

The sun dipped low, painting the tents gold.

Canvas snapped in the evening wind. Cooking fires crackled. The women moved with quiet efficiency, stirring pots, rolling out bedding, checking knots on tent ropes. They were tired—but strong. This was the kind of tired that meant something was built.

From the ridge, the men returned.

Not on horses this time.

On foot.

Slow.

Uncertain.

Preston cleared his throat. "Ladies..."

No one turned.

Marisol kept stirring the pot.

Millicent folded blankets.

Moonland checked the fire.

Paxton swallowed. "We... want to talk."

Magnolia finally turned.

Her face was calm.

But her eyes were steel.

"You had your chance to talk," she said. "Today is about work."

Phoenix stepped forward. "We've been praying."

Marigold snorted. "Prayer without action is just noise."

Silence fell.

The Scripture

Magnolia reached into her satchel and pulled out her Bible.

She opened it slowly.

"Ephesians 5:25," she said.

Her voice carried.

"Husbands, love your wives, just as Christ loved the church and gave himself up for her."

She closed the book.

"That means sacrifice."

"Protection."

"Provision."

"Consistency."

"Not just words."

Marisol added, "Christ didn't just talk."

"He died."

Millicent snapped, "What have y'all sacrificed for us?"

The men stared at their boots.

The Men Try Again

Preston stepped closer.

"I know we messed up."

Magnolia cut him off.

"Saying it ain't enough."

Parker spoke. "We were scared."

Moonland replied, "So were we."

Paxton swallowed. "We didn't know how to act."

Marisol snapped, "You knew how to fight."

"You knew how to tie us up."

"You knew how to throw us in wagons."

"So don't tell me you don't know how to try."

Phoenix's eyes filled.

"That night... in jail... when you kept us warm..."

Moonland held up a hand.

"That wasn't romance."

"That was survival., you just want to sleep with us not love us"

Silence again.

Emotional Vulnerability

Pablo finally broke.

"I never had a home," he said quietly. "Rail life... it raised me."

"I don't know how to build a family."

Marisol looked at him.

Softened—just a little.

"Then learn."

"But not on our backs."

Pierce whispered, "My daddy drank."

"I swore I'd be different."

Millicent crossed her arms.

"Different requires effort."

"Not promises."

Porter said, "I'm scared of failing you."

Margaret replied softly, "Failing us would be not trying."

Tears slipped from Paxton's eyes.

"I never been chosen."

Marigold tilted her head.

"Then start choosing."

"Every day."

The Women Draw the Line

Magnolia stepped forward.

"We prefer not to deal with you right now."

The words were firm.

Not cruel.

"We're healing."

"We're building."

"We don't need men who just talk."

Millicent added, "Words don't cook."

"They don't build."

"They don't protect."

Marisol snapped, "Y'all still lazy."

Paxton flinched.

Phoenix frowned. "That hurts."

Magnolia replied, "Truth hurts before it heals."

Faith Without Works

Moonland spoke quietly.

"James 2:17."

"Faith by itself, if it is not accompanied by action, is dead."

She met their eyes.

"Your love is dead if it don't move."

The men stood still.

Humbled.

The Rejection

Parker tried one last time.

"We just wanna be near you."

Millicent shook her head.

"Near ain't enough, you just want someone to sleep with."

"Present ain't enough."

"Choose us."

"Daily."

Marisol added, "You still strangers."

"Not trust."

Preston swallowed.

"What do we do?"

Magnolia looked at him.

"Become men worth following."

They Walk Away

The women turned.

Back to their tents.

Their fires.

Their plans.

No glances back.

No tears.

They chose themselves tonight.

The Men Left Standing

Paxton whispered, "They don't need us."

Phoenix said, "They deserve better."

Parker nodded. "We gotta earn it."

Preston clenched his jaw.

"I will."

Women's Prayer

Inside the main tent, the women joined hands.

"Lord," Magnolia whispered, "teach us patience."

"Teach us wisdom."

"Teach us when to walk away."

"And when to stand."

Marisol added, "We refuse to settle."

Millicent said, "We deserve more."

Moonland whispered, "We trust You."

They all said, "Amen."

Outside, the men watched the tent lights glow.

Inside, the women laughed softly.

Safe.

Strong.

Unmoved.

Not yet.

Night Work and Quiet Watchers

The fire had burned low.

Ash glowed red under the stars, and the smell of cooked beans still hung in the air. The women moved with practiced hands, stamping out embers with their boots, scattering dirt over coals, making sure nothing could spark back to life.

"No loose ends," Magnolia said. "We don't build just to burn it down."

Marisol kicked the last ember. "Fire's dead."

Millicent gathered plates. "Wipe the table."

Moonland folded the canvas cover. "Tools secured."

Margaret checked the tent lines. "Everything tight."

Miyako nodded. "Clean site."

Marigold laughed. "Men would've left it smoking."

They cleaned in silence, tired but satisfied.

No rush. No fear.

Work finished properly.

Leaving the Land

The wagons were waiting.

Horses snorted softly in the dark. The women climbed up one by one, skirts pulled aside, boots settling into place.

Magnolia took the reins.

"Back to the boardinghouse."

Millicent sighed. "Hot bath."

Marisol grinned. "Sleep."

Moonland whispered, "Tomorrow we build again."

They rolled out.

Wheels creaked. Lanterns bobbed. The tents stood quiet behind them, proof of what they had done without permission.

Unseen Protectors

Up on the ridge, two men watched.

Preston Protect. Phoenix Protect.

They hadn't spoken about it.

They just... did it.

Preston adjusted his hat. "They shouldn't ride alone."

Phoenix nodded. "Not after today."

"They told us to leave them alone," Preston said.

Phoenix replied, "Protection ain't possession."

Preston mounted his horse.

"Quiet."

Phoenix followed.

They stayed back.

Far enough not to be seen. Close enough to act.

Not controlling. Watching.

On the Road

In the wagon, Marisol leaned back.

"Today felt good."

Millicent nodded. "We did something real."

Moonland added, "And we didn't fold."

Magnolia smiled faintly. "Boundaries feel powerful."

Margaret whispered, "They don't own us."

Miyako said, "And we don't need to explain."

Marigold laughed. "Let them be confused."

They didn't know they were being followed.

Nor would they have wanted to.

Men in the Shadows

Phoenix slowed his horse when the wagon slowed.

Preston whispered, "They look tired."

"Good tired," Phoenix said. "Earned tired."

They watched shadows move inside the wagon.

Laughter drifted back.

Preston swallowed. "They don't laugh with us like that."

Phoenix replied, "Not yet."

Silence fell.

They rode on.

A Close Call

A rustle came from the brush.

Phoenix tensed.

Preston's hand moved to his belt.

A coyote darted out and disappeared.

Phoenix exhaled.

"They safe."

Preston nodded.

"Good."

Arrival

The boardinghouse lights glowed ahead.

Magnolia pulled the wagon to a stop.

They climbed down, stretching tired limbs.

Millicent sighed. "Home."

Marisol laughed. "For now."

They went inside.

Door closed.

Warmth.

Safety.

Men Pull Back

Phoenix slowed.

Preston stopped.

They didn't go any closer.

"That's far enough," Phoenix said.

Preston nodded.

"They told us to give space."

"We did," Phoenix replied. "And we still watched."

Preston looked at the window where the light glowed.

"I don't want to lose her."

Phoenix said quietly, "Then become the man she'd choose."

They turned their horses.

Rode back into the dark.

Not victorious. Not defeated.

Committed.

Inside the Boardinghouse

Magnolia removed her hat.

Millicent kicked off her boots.

Marisol laughed. "I'm sore."

Moonland smiled. "Good sore."

Margaret stretched. "We earned rest."

Miyako said, "And tomorrow we build again."

Marigold clapped. "Same energy."

They headed upstairs.

Not knowing they had been guarded.

Not needing to know.

Because they were learning to stand on their own.

Chapter Eight

Men Who Don't Know How to Win

The men didn't know what to do.

That truth sat heavy on their chests every morning when they saddled their horses and rode toward the ranch. They were strong men. Former rail police. Men who had faced bandits, storms, blood, and danger.

But these women?

They were powerful in a way the men had never known.

They didn't fold under pressure. They didn't retreat. They didn't soften because of fear.

They stood straight in storms.

Preston Protect watched Magnolia from the ridge every morning. She moved like a commander, pointing, directing, lifting, carrying. Her fitted pants hugged her strength, wide belt resting firm at her waist, her billowing shirt catching the wind like a banner.

Phoenix watched Moonland bend to lift a beam, muscles tightening in her arms, her braid swinging down her back. She didn't ask for help. She didn't need permission.

Parker stared too long at Millicent adjusting her gloves, rolling up her sleeves, her movements confident and graceful. He felt something shift inside him — a pull he didn't understand.

Paxton groaned under his breath watching Marigold climb onto the wagon, one boot on the wheel, the other swinging up. The way she moved stirred something dangerous in him.

Pablo couldn't look away from Marisol's laugh, her hips swaying as she carried crates. He imagined pulling her close and instantly felt ashamed.

Porter noticed Margaret's quiet strength — how she bent low to scrub, then stood straight again without complaint. His chest tightened.

Pierce watched Miyako walk across the field, posture perfect, chin lifted, eyes alert. He thought, I don't deserve her.

Desire Without Permission

The men had never been trained for this kind of battle.

Desire.

Not lust — but longing.

They wanted to:

hold their wives • smell their hair • wrap arms around them • feel warmth • steal one quiet moment

But they hadn't earned one hour of that.

Preston clenched his jaw. "I want to touch her," he admitted quietly. "But I don't deserve it."

Phoenix nodded. "They know more about closeness than we do."

Parker sighed. "They trained."

Paxton muttered, "They lived."

Silence fell.

None of them truly knew their wives' pasts. Not fully. They guessed. They felt it in their bones — these women had lived hard.

Pablo whispered, "They probably know more about touch than we ever will."

Porter added, "And they chose God anyway."

Pierce exhaled. "That takes strength."

The Confession

They gathered near the fence one afternoon.

Sweat on brows. Dust on boots.

Paxton blurted, "We need help."

Everyone looked at him.

"I don't know how to win her," he said. "I don't know how to love a woman like that."

Phoenix nodded. "Me neither."

Parker sighed. "I don't want to scare her."

Preston said quietly, "I don't want to own her."

They all stood silent.

Pablo finally said, "We go see the Reverend."

The Reverend

Reverend James Carter sat behind his desk, Bible open.

He studied them.

"You married?"

They nodded.

"By force," Paxton admitted.

The reverend sighed. "God don't waste situations."

Preston leaned forward. "We don't know how to win them."

Reverend Carter smiled gently. "You don't win women."

"You serve them."

Silence.

Phoenix frowned. "Serve?"

"Yes," the reverend said. "Jesus served."

"Loved without control."

"Protected without possession."

"Sacrificed."

Parker swallowed. "They don't trust us."

Reverend nodded. "Trust is built with actions."

"Not flowers." "Not speeches." "Consistency."

Paxton whispered, "They ignore us."

"Good," the reverend replied. "That means you start from zero."

Meeting the Judge

They went to Judge Whitmore next.

He leaned back in his chair, amused.

"Y'all want marriage advice from the man who forced you to marry?"

"Yes, sir," Preston said.

Judge chuckled. "Serves me right."

Phoenix said, "They don't trust us."

Judge nodded. "Would you?"

Silence.

"Show up," the judge said. "Don't speak."

206

"Work."

"Protect."

"Leave when asked."

"Repeat."

Paxton scratched his head. "That's it?"

Judge smiled. "That's everything."

They Try Again — Through Action

The next morning...

The men didn't approach.

They didn't speak.

They just worked.

They fixed broken fences.

They hauled lumber.

They repaired wagon wheels.

They mended torn canvas.

They didn't ask permission.

They didn't expect praise.

They worked until hands blistered.

Women Still Ignore Them

Marisol noticed.

Said nothing.

Millicent watched.

Said nothing.

Magnolia saw Preston carrying heavy beams.

She didn't stop him.

She didn't thank him.

She didn't soften.

Moonland observed Phoenix repairing tent stakes.

No words.

Margaret watched Porter bring water for the crew.

She didn't smile.

Miyako saw Pierce hauling dirt.

No reaction.

Marigold saw Paxton working until he staggered.

She said nothing.

The men kept working.

Unexpected Kindness

Then it happened.

Not from the women.

From the crew.

Señor Alvarez handed Preston water.

"You good man," he said.

Preston nodded.

Pablo helped one worker lift a crate.

"Gracias."

"De nada."

Small kindnesses.

Not from wives.

But from strangers.

It humbled them.

Trust Tested

Later, a rail man rode in.

Offered money.

"Walk away," he said.

Preston didn't hesitate.

"No."

Phoenix stepped forward.

"Get off this land."

The man laughed.

"Your wives don't even talk to you."

Paxton snapped, "That don't mean we sell them out."

The man rode off.

The women watched.

Still silent.

But they saw.

God Moving Quietly

That night...

Magnolia whispered to Millicent, "They worked today."

Millicent replied, "Didn't ask."

Marisol smiled faintly. "They learning."

Moonland said softly, "God moving."

Margaret nodded. "Slow."

Miyako whispered, "But real."

Marigold smirked. "Still ain't forgiven them."

They laughed.

Men Alone

By the fire that night...

Paxton whispered, "They didn't thank us."

Phoenix replied, "They don't owe us."

Parker nodded. "We doing this for us."

Preston stared at the stars.

"I'm gonna be a man she'd choose."

Silence.

Hope.

Across the field, the women laughed quietly.

The men listened.

Not approaching.

Not demanding.

Just learning.

For the first time...

They were becoming men worth loving.

Wanting What You Haven't Earned

The women still ignored them.

Not cruelly. Not loudly. Just... completely.

No greetings. No glances. No small talk.

If the men passed close by, the women moved around them like wind around a fence post—acknowledging the space but not the person.

It hurt.

More than punches. More than mud fights. More than the courtroom humiliation.

Silence cut deeper.

The men went back to their own land

They couldn't linger.

Cattle needed water. Sheep needed tending. Fences still needed fixing.

So they returned to their portion of the land.

Work didn't care about heartbreak.

Preston shoveled feed with his jaw tight. Phoenix checked hooves. Paxton wrestled a stubborn gate. Parker repaired a split rail. Pierce hauled hay. Porter mended rope. Pablo fixed a broken trough.

Sweat poured.

But their eyes kept drifting to the distance.

Where the women worked.

Where laughter rose.

Where strength moved freely.

Watching from Afar

Preston leaned on his shovel.

Magnolia bent to lift a crate.

Her belt hugged her waist. Her pants stretched with movement. Her shirt floated in the breeze.

His chest tightened.

Lord... help me.

Phoenix swallowed watching Moonland stretch her arms, braid swinging down her back. She moved like she knew exactly who she was.

Parker couldn't look away from Millicent when she laughed—head tilted back, eyes bright, hands on her hips like she owned the land beneath her feet.

Paxton watched Marigold jump off the wagon. One boot hit ground, then the other. Strong. Confident.

Pablo's heart raced when Marisol wiped sweat from her neck. He imagined brushing that hair back and instantly felt ashamed.

Porter watched Margaret kneel to scrub something from her hands. Her sleeves rolled, wrists slim but strong.

Pierce noticed Miyako walk the fence line, straight-backed, eyes scanning like a hawk.

They all felt it.

Desire.

Not just physical.

But closeness. Warmth. Belonging.

Confession Among Men

That night, near their fire, Paxton broke.

"I need her," he said quietly.

Everyone looked up.

"I don't just want her," he added. "I need her."

Silence.

Phoenix nodded slowly. "Me too."

Parker swallowed. "I want to hold my wife. Smell her hair. Sleep knowing she safe."

Pierce muttered, "I don't know how to ask."

Porter stared at flames. "I don't deserve it."

Pablo whispered, "They don't trust us."

Preston clenched his jaw. "They shouldn't."

Physical Honesty

Paxton rubbed his neck.

"I'm gonna say something real."

Everyone listened.

"I'm a man. I desire my wife., and I want to sleep beside her every night."

No one laughed.

Phoenix nodded. "That's honest."

"I want to kiss her," Paxton said. "Hold her."

"But I ain't earned that."

Silence.

Parker whispered, "I get so distracted watching her work... I forget my own."

Porter exhaled. "It's like God woke something in me."

Pierce said quietly, "I never wanted to touch a woman respectfully before."

They sat with that.

Working Through It

They worked harder.

Longer.

Without being seen.

They dug a trench that didn't need digging. Fixed fence that wasn't broken. Cleaned stalls twice.

Not to impress.

To redirect their desire.

Phoenix said quietly, "Work it out."

Women Still Ignore Them

The next day...

Same silence.

Marisol walked past Pablo like he was air.

Millicent didn't acknowledge Parker bringing water.

Magnolia didn't thank Preston for clearing a path.

Moonland stepped around Phoenix.

Marigold pretended Paxton didn't exist.

Margaret walked by Porter.

Miyako passed Pierce.

No cruelty.

Just distance.

The Weight of It

Preston rode back to his land heavy.

"She don't even look at me."

Phoenix nodded. "She protecting her heart."

Parker sighed. "She owes me nothing."

Paxton whispered, "I'm tired of wanting what I can't touch."

Silence.

God in the Quiet

That night, Preston knelt alone.

"Lord... I'm a man."

"I feel things."

"But I don't want to be like before."

"Teach me control."

"Teach me patience."

Across the land...

Phoenix prayed. "Make me worthy."

Parker prayed. "Make me gentle."

Paxton prayed. "Make me better."

Women Talking

At the boardinghouse, the women whispered.

"They working," Millicent said.

Marisol shrugged. "Good."

Moonland said quietly, "They watching us."

Margaret replied, "Let them."

Miyako nodded. "We're not ready."

Marigold smirked. "They thirsty."

Magnolia smiled faintly. "Let them grow."

They Need Them

Back at the ranch...

Paxton groaned. "We need them."

219

Phoenix nodded. "Not just want."

"They smart," Parker said. "They see things we miss."

Preston swallowed. "They would've built better."

Pablo whispered, "They make life... better."

A rail man rode up early one morning.

"Still ignoring you, huh?"

Paxton clenched his fist. "We choose them."

"Funny," the man sneered. "They don't choose you."

Phoenix stepped forward. "Get off our land."

The man laughed and left.

Women See It

Marigold watched from afar.

"They didn't sell out."

Magnolia nodded. "They choosing right."

Night Thoughts

That night...

Preston stared at stars.

"I want to be chosen."

Phoenix replied, "Then stay steady."

Paxton whispered, "I want her arms around me."

Parker added, "I want her trust."

Porter murmured, "I want her peace."

Pierce said quietly, "I want her smile."

They sat in silence.

Wanting.

Waiting.

God Working Quietly

Not with lightning.

Not with thunder.

But with:

restraint • patience • consistency • sweat •
silence

God was shaping men.

Slowly.

Across the land, Magnolia lay in bed.

She whispered, "They trying."

Millicent replied, "Still too early."

Marisol smiled. "But they changing."

Moonland said softly, "God working."

And the men...

Fell asleep.

Alone.

But not hopeless.

For the first time...

They wanted to be worthy.

Not just wanted.

Chapter Nine

Near... But Not Yet

For several days, the men stayed away.

Not out of anger. Not out of pride. Out of respect.

They worked their land from dawn to dusk and avoided the tents where the women built their future. No passing by. No pretending to need tools. No wandering glances.

They gave space.

And it nearly broke them.

Church Day

Sunday came soft and bright.

The bell rang.

Boots moved. Hats lifted. Bibles tucked under arms.

And then...

The women entered.

Oh my goodness.

Every man forgot how to breathe.

224

Magnolia in a soft cream dress, waist fitted, skirt flowing. Millicent in deep blue, gloves delicate, hair pinned high. Marisol in warm brown silk, eyes shining. Moonland in pale green, serene and glowing. Margaret in lavender, gentle and radiant. Miyako in ivory with lace trim, elegant. Marigold in golden yellow, smiling like sunshine.

They looked like royalty.

Not flashy. Not loud. Just... beautiful.

The men sat straight.

Hands clenched.

Eyes forward.

Trying not to stare.

Trying not to fail.

Still Ignored

The women didn't look at them.

Not once.

They sat together.

Prayed together.

Sang together.

The men could feel them near...

But unreachable.

Paxton whispered, "Lord help me."

Phoenix swallowed. "They stunning."

Parker exhaled, "How she do that to me?"

Preston clenched his jaw. "I don't deserve this view."

Sunday Tea

After service, the women returned to their tents.

They set out tea. Fresh bread. Crumpets. Honey.

Laughter floated.

The men watched from a distance.

Not approaching.

Just observing.

Magnolia lifted her teacup. Millicent laughed. Marisol leaned back in her chair. Moonland closed her eyes in peace.

A soft breeze moved their dresses.

The men sat on their horses.

Helpless.

The Tease

And then it happened.

Slowly.

One by one.

Subtle.

Magnolia adjusted her collar... just a little lower.

Not indecent.

Just enough to show her graceful neckline.

Millicent loosened her gloves and rolled her sleeves up slightly.

Marisol brushed her hair aside, exposing her neck.

Moonland let her collar slip just enough.

Margaret shifted her shawl.

Miyako adjusted the lace at her throat.

Marigold stretched, neckline dipping a whisper.

The men froze.

Eyes widened.

Heat spread.

Paxton turned his horse away fast. "Lord have mercy."

Phoenix covered his mouth. "They playing with fire."

Parker laughed nervously. "They trained."

Preston shut his eyes. "God help me."

They turned.

Rode back toward their ranch.

Trying to act strong.

Women See Them Leave

From the tents...

The women noticed.

Marisol laughed softly. "Did you see that?"

Millicent grinned. "They ran."

Magnolia smiled knowingly.

Moonland whispered, "They still want."

Margaret adjusted her collar back up. "Good."

Miyako nodded. "Not yet."

Marigold laughed. "They ain't earned that view yet."

They pulled their sleeves back up.

Covered themselves.

Trained.

Controlled.

Available only to husbands...

But husbands had to earn it.

Men Complaining

Back at the ranch...

Paxton groaned. "They teasing us."

Phoenix laughed. "On purpose."

Parker shook his head. "They dangerous."

Pierce muttered, "My heart can't take it."

Porter sighed. "I wanted to ride back."

Preston clenched his fists. "They testing us."

Paxton said, "And we failing."

Phoenix replied, "No... we leaving."

"That's growth."

The Prayer

They gathered in the old living room.

Dusty.

Rough furniture.

But sincere hearts.

Paxton knelt. "Lord… help me not to rush."

Phoenix prayed. "Teach me patience."

Parker whispered. "Make me worthy."

Pierce said, "Help me respect her."

Porter bowed. "Guard my eyes."

Pablo sighed. "Help me control my flesh."

Preston finished. "Make me a husband she'd choose."

Silence followed.

Peace settled.

Women Praying Too

At the tents…

Magnolia whispered, "Lord… we feel it too."

Millicent nodded. "Desire."

Marisol smiled softly. "But we waiting."

Moonland said, "Guard our hearts."

Margaret added, "Help us not manipulate."

Miyako whispered, "Keep us pure."

Marigold laughed quietly. "Even when we tease."

They all smiled.

Across the land...

Men prayed. Women prayed.

Longing sat between them.

Not acted on.

Not rushed.

Just... present.

And God...

God smiled.

Because discipline was being learned.

And love was being built...

Not rushed.

Three Months of Silence

Nearly three months had passed.

Three months of dust. Hammering.
Blueprints. Orders. Deliveries.

And the women never slowed.

From dawn until the sun dipped low,
Magnolia, Millicent, Marisol, Moonland,
Margaret, Miyako, and Marigold moved
through the construction site like generals.

At least 100 workers filled the land now.

Carpenters. Plaster men. Stone masons.
Painters. Floor layers.

The women knew every name.

Every schedule.

Every shipment.

Magnolia stood with a clipboard. "Kitchen
stoves arriving Tuesday."

Millicent flipped pages. "Beds for fifteen
bedrooms confirmed."

Marisol smiled. "Curtains ordered."

Moonland nodded. "Towels and linens."

Margaret added, "Pots and pans."

Miyako checked a list. "Wash tubs."

Marigold laughed. "Lord... we building a palace."

And they were.

The House

The house was massive.

Two full wash rooms with coiled tubs. A grand parlor with tall windows. Two huge kitchens—one for daily use, one for community cooking. Wide staircases. Long hallways. Fifteen bedrooms.

It was beautiful.

Not fancy. Strong.

Built to last.

Built for families.

Built for purpose.

Magnolia whispered one afternoon, "If we'd left this to them…"

Millicent finished, "We'd still be sleeping in tents."

They laughed.

Their Plan

The men stayed away.

Not because the women asked.

Because the men chose to.

They didn't bring a single cow near the house.

Didn't ride close.

Didn't pretend to help.

They worked their land instead.

The women noticed.

And they didn't mind.

It was part of the plan.

Marisol whispered one night, "They gotta want us."

Millicent nodded. "For who we are."

Moonland said quietly, "Not because a judge said."

Magnolia added, "Marriage without choice is a prison."

Church Still Hurts

Sunday still came.

And the men still saw them.

Still beautiful.

Still distant.

They sat apart.

They didn't walk together.

Didn't whisper.

Didn't share hymn books.

After service...

They passed on the grounds.

Just a nod.

Nothing else.

Preston whispered once, "Good morning."

Magnolia nodded.

No words.

Paxton nodded to Marigold.

She nodded back.

Nothing else.

Phoenix tried to smile at Moonland.

She looked past him.

Parker sighed.

"This is torture."

Pain in Silence

The men broke.

Not publicly.

Privately.

Paxton knelt by his bed. "I don't deserve her."

Phoenix stared at the ceiling. "I miss her laugh."

Parker whispered, "I want her to look at me."

Pierce cried quietly. "I don't know how to fix this."

Porter clenched his fists. "I hate who I was."

Pablo sighed. "I want her to trust me."

Preston whispered, "I want to be chosen."

They prayed.

Every night.

Not for bodies.

For hearts.

Desire Is Heavy

They could barely look at the women.

Their beauty hurt.

The way Magnolia stood tall. Millicent's laugh. Marisol's eyes. Moonland's calm. Margaret's grace. Miyako's quiet strength. Marigold's fire.

Their fitted pants.

Their wide belts.

Their confidence.

It stirred things the men had never learned to control.

Paxton whispered, "I can't even look at her without wanting to hold her."

Phoenix nodded. "That's why I look away."

Parker sighed, "I don't trust myself yet."

God Working Quietly

The women noticed the change.

Less anger.

More humility.

Magnolia whispered to Millicent, "They praying."

Millicent nodded. "I see it."

Marisol said, "They don't chase us."

Moonland smiled. "That's growth."

Margaret whispered, "They respecting boundaries."

Miyako added, "That's rare."

Marigold laughed. "They hurting."

But her eyes softened.

Moving Day Nears

One afternoon, Magnolia read the list aloud.

"Beds arriving Thursday."

"Kitchen stoves Friday."

"Furniture Saturday."

Millicent smiled. "We move in next week."

The women stopped.

Looked around.

The house was real now.

Walls. Windows. Floors.

Marisol whispered, "We did this."

Moonland nodded. "With God."

Men Watching from Afar

From their portioned land...

The men watched wagons roll.

Furniture.

Bedding.

Curtains.

Phoenix whispered, "They really did it."

Paxton nodded. "They don't need us."

Parker swallowed. "They wanted us to want them."

Preston said quietly, "And now we do."

Painful Growth

Paxton admitted, "I've never waited this long for a woman."

Phoenix said, "I've never been denied."

Parker laughed softly. "I deserve it."

Porter whispered, "They making men out of us."

At night, Magnolia sat on the porch of the new house.

She whispered, "Lord... we waited."

Millicent joined her. "They changing."

Marisol smiled. "Slow."

Moonland nodded. "But real."

They watched the stars.

Across the land...

Preston knelt.

"Lord... I still want her."

"But I want to be worthy more."

Silence.

Peace.

Hope.

When Walls Finally Came Down**

Moving day arrived like a whirlwind.

Wagons lined the drive. Crates. Furniture. Rugs. Mirrors. Boxes of china. Bundles of curtains.

The women directed everything.

"Bed in that corner." "Curtains go there." "Wash tubs upstairs." "Pots in the big kitchen."

By nightfall, they were exhausted.

Magnolia sank onto the edge of her bed and laughed. "I can't move."

Millicent kicked off her boots. "I'm sleeping for a year."

Marisol groaned. "My arms are done."

Moonland smiled. "Worth it."

Margaret whispered, "This house is beautiful."

Miyako said softly, "God did this."

Marigold laughed. "And we did too."

They slept.

Hard.

Two full days.

Not stirring. Not talking. Just resting.

Waking Up to Victory

The Celebration

That night, they celebrated properly.

A long table.

Roasted chicken. Buttered potatoes. Corn on the cob. Fresh rolls. Cakes. Pies.

Marigold leaned back. "I'm full-full."

Marisol laughed. "Food victory."

Moonland smiled. "This house deserved a feast."

They cleaned up and agreed.

"Early bed."

It was still hot outside, so they slipped into thin night clothes. Soft cotton. Light fabric. Hair loose. Bare feet.

Each bedroom was stunning.

Carved beds. Fresh linens. Soft rugs. Wash bowls.

They crawled into bed grateful.

The men still hadn't been invited.

This was their space.

The Knock

Late.

Hard.

Knocking.

Every woman froze.

Magnolia reached under her pillow and pulled out the rifle.

Millicent grabbed the pistol she kept near.

Marisol whispered, "Who is it?"

Magnolia opened the door just enough to see.

Seven men stood there.

Their husbands.

Nervous. Tired. Serious.

Preston cleared his throat. "Can we come in? We need to talk."

The women looked at each other.

Moonland said, "Separate rooms. Doors stay open."

They stepped aside.

Barefoot. Hair down. Robes pulled tight.

The men swallowed hard.

They had never seen them like this.

Soft. Natural. Real.

Private Rooms

Each wife led her husband to her room.

And one by one...

Each man closed the door.

Not locking.

Just privacy.

Preston stood awkwardly.

"I need to ask you something," he whispered.

Magnolia crossed her arms. "What?"

"Will you... kiss me?"

She raised a brow. "Why?"

"Because I need it," he said quietly. "I been holding everything in."

She studied him.

Then leaned in.

A slow kiss.

Not rushed. Not playful.

Real.

Preston exhaled like he had been underwater for six months.

In Every Room

Same story.

Paxton whispered, "I need to feel you."

Marigold smirked. "Why?"

"Because I choose you."

She kissed him.

Phoenix said, "I don't want jail marriage."

"I want you."

Moonland searched his face.

Then kissed him.

Parker cried. "I want my wife."

Millicent hugged him tight before kissing him.

Every man said the same thing.

"I'm not leaving till morning."

They had planned it.

The Real Questions

But the women made them talk first.

"Do you want me... or convenience?" "Did you choose me?" "Or are you scared to be alone?"

Men broke.

Tears.

"I want you." "I choose you." "I've always wanted you."

No pride.

No bravado.

Just truth.

Morning

Morning came.

And every man was worn out.

Not from sin.

From emotion. Tears. Truth. Closeness.

The women laughed.

"Stay in bed," Magnolia ordered.

"We cooking."

They padded to the kitchen.

Still in robes.

Laughing.

Marigold teased, "If they get brave and come unannounced again..."

Millicent laughed. "We gonna wear them out again."

Marisol added, "That's what they get."

Moonland smiled. "God ordained."

Margaret nodded. "The marriage bed is undefiled."

249

Miyako giggled. "They didn't expect that."

They laughed louder.

Breakfast in Bed

They carried trays upstairs.

Bacon. Eggs. Biscuits. Gravy.

Men groaned.

"Don't move," Magnolia teased. "You earned rest."

Paxton laughed. "I can't feel my legs."

Marigold winked. "Good."

They ate slowly.

Smiling.

Not rushing.

No labels.

No pressure.

Just... closeness.

And the women laughed again.

"That's what y'all get for coming unannounced."

Men Who Were Not Ready for That Kind of Love

The men gathered at their ranch just before sunrise.

They sat on crates. On fence posts. On overturned buckets.

Every single one of them looked worn out.

Not dirty. Not beaten.

Just... drained.

Emotionally. Physically. Spiritually.

Paxton rubbed his face. "I don't know what just happened to me."

Phoenix laughed weakly. "Same."

Parker shook his head slowly. "Those women... Lord."

Pierce leaned back. "They planned that."

Porter groaned. "Every bit of it."

Pablo sighed. "They ain't random."

Preston sat quiet, staring into the distance.

"They knew exactly what they were doing."
252

Comparing Notes

Paxton broke the silence.

"Those wives use every romantic way to love?"

Phoenix laughed. "Every single one."

Parker nodded. "I thought I was ready."

Pierce muttered, "I was not ready."

Porter leaned forward. "They didn't rush."

"They took their time."

"They looked at you."

"They listened."

"They asked questions."

Paxton groaned. "That part got me."

Pablo shook his head. "She made me talk."

Phoenix added, "They made us confess."

Preston finally spoke.

"She didn't just touch me."

"She saw me."

Silence fell.

They Knew It Was Planned

Paxton laughed.

"They had it mapped out."

Phoenix nodded. "Same questions."

Parker snapped his fingers. "Same order."

"They hugged first," Pierce said. "Then kissed."

"Then made you talk," Porter added.

Pablo sighed. "And when you tried to move fast…"

"She slowed you down," Phoenix said.

Paxton groaned. "Too smooth."

They all laughed weakly.

Spiritually, Legally, Physically

Parker leaned back.

"Now we married in every way."

Spiritually. Legally. Physically.

"And I don't know what to do."

Preston whispered, "I thought I'd feel powerful."

Paxton laughed. "I feel humbled."

Phoenix nodded. "They flipped the script."

"They led."

"They controlled the pace."

Pierce added, "And somehow made it feel safe."

Porter exhaled. "That's rare."

Over-Satisfied

Paxton rubbed his shoulders.

"I'm sore."

Pablo groaned. "My legs don't work."

Phoenix laughed. "I slept like a rock."

Parker sighed. "I didn't even dream."

Preston shook his head.

"I feel... full."

Not food.

Not pride.

Content.

Satisfied.

Emotional Fallout

Paxton got quiet.

"I cried."

Phoenix looked up.

"So did I."

Pierce admitted, "I told her stuff I never told nobody."

Porter nodded. "She made me feel seen."

Pablo whispered, "I didn't know love could feel like that."

Preston said softly, "She didn't take from me."

"She gave."

Silence.

Men swallowing emotions.

Now What?

Paxton finally said it.

"So what we do now?"

Phoenix shrugged. "Keep earning."

Parker nodded. "They didn't say everything fixed."

Pierce added, "They still watching us."

Porter said, "They still choosing."

Preston stood.

"Then we choose back."

Respect Grows

Paxton said, "I ain't ever met women like them."

Phoenix smiled. "They dangerous."

Parker laughed. "In a good way."

Pierce nodded. "They strong."

Porter added, "They smart."

Pablo whispered, "They saved."

Preston finished.

"They ours... but not owned."

God's Hand

Phoenix stared at the sky.

"That was God."

Paxton nodded. "Had to be."

Parker whispered, "He knew we needed that."

Pierce added, "To break us."

Porter said, "To rebuild us."

Preston closed his eyes.

"Thank You, Lord."

The Women Watching

From the porch...

Magnolia saw them sitting together.

Talking.

Laughing weakly.

She smiled.

Millicent leaned beside her.

"They look tired."

Marisol laughed. "Good."

Moonland smiled. "They needed it."

Margaret nodded. "God used us."

Miyako giggled. "They thought they were in control."

Marigold smirked. "They met generals."

They laughed quietly.

Paxton stood.

"We better get to work."

Phoenix groaned. "After some coffee."

They all laughed.

Preston looked back toward the house.

"I ain't never running from her again."

The men mounted their horses.

Not swaggering.

Not bragging.

Changed.

Because love had touched them.

259

Chapter Ten

When Other Men Come Calling

The rumors started quietly.

Whispers at the feed store. Murmurs outside the post office. Side glances in church.

"They don't even live with their husbands." "Strange marriages." "Those women running their own ranch."

And then it changed.

Rival ranchers began to notice.

Not just the land. Not just the business success.

The women.

The Offers Begin

One afternoon, Magnolia was checking deliveries when a tall rancher rode up.

He removed his hat slowly.

"Ma'am," he said smoothly, "name's Everett Boone."

She looked up, unimpressed. "What do you need?"

He smiled. "I heard you're a smart businesswoman."

"True," she said.

"I own land west of here," he continued. "Good pasture. Better water than this side."

She folded her arms. "And?"

"I'd like to partner."

She raised an eyebrow.

"Partner how?"

"Money," he said. "Expansion."

"Protection."

"And... well," he hesitated, "Companionship."

She stared at him.

"I'm married."

He shrugged.

"You don't live with him."

Her eyes hardened.

261

"Leave."

They All Try

Millicent received silk scarves.

Marisol got fresh flowers.

Moonland received a fine saddle.

Margaret was offered shares in cattle.

Miyako got a gold brooch.

Marigold received a diamond ring.

Each man said the same thing.

"You deserve better." "He can't provide." "I'll take care of you."

Some added:

"Spiritually." "Physically." "Every way."

The women were stunned.

Then angry.

The Husbands Find Out

Phoenix heard it first.

Two ranchers at the saloon.

"They trying to steal their wives." "Because they don't live with them."

Paxton slammed his glass down.

"They better stop."

Parker swallowed.

"They think we incompetent."

Pierce muttered.

"They think we slackers."

Porter clenched his jaw.

"They think we weak."

Pablo whispered.

"They think we cowards."

Preston stood.

"We will not lose them."

The Rumors Grow

By the next day, the gossip spread.

"They don't satisfy their wives." "They got nothing to offer." "They scared to lead." "They let women run everything."

The men heard it all.

Every word.

It cut deep.

Paxton whispered, "They attacking our manhood."

Phoenix replied, "They attacking our covenant."

Watching the Suitors

The husbands began watching.

Ranchers rode in daily.

Sometimes alone. Sometimes in pairs.

Bringing gifts.

Trying smiles.

The men watched from afar.

Fists clenched.

Teeth gritted.

Preston whispered, "They bold."

Parker muttered, "Disrespectful."

Phoenix said quietly, "They think we won't fight."

Women's Response

That evening, the women gathered.

Magnolia slammed a letter down.

"They think we for sale."

Marisol scoffed.

"They think we lonely."

Millicent shook her head.

"They think we weak."

Moonland said softly.

"They don't know us."

Margaret whispered.

"We're married."

Miyako nodded.

"By choice now."

Marigold grinned.

"And we loyal."

They laughed.

The Test of Loyalty

The next day...

A wealthy rancher approached Marigold.

"Your husband can't give you this," he said, holding out papers.

Land deeds.

She laughed.

"My husband gives me something you never could."

"What's that?" he asked.

"Respect."

She walked away.

Men Struggle

That night, the husbands sat silent.

Preston whispered, "They want what's ours."

Phoenix replied, "They see gold."

Paxton added, "They don't see covenant."

Parker swallowed.

"They think we not enough."

Preston stood.

"Then we prove we are."

God Speaks Quietly

Phoenix opened his Bible.

"Proverbs 31," he read. "Her husband trusts in her, and he will have no lack of gain."

They sat with that.

"She trusts us," Paxton whispered.

"Then we protect," Preston said.

A New Resolve

The men decided:

No fighting. No threats. No boasting.

They would show:

Consistency • Leadership • Provision • Protection • Respect

Not for pride.

For covenant.

From her porch, Magnolia watched Preston standing guard near the fence line.

He wasn't hovering.

He wasn't interfering.

Just... present.

She smiled softly.

Across the land...

The battle wasn't about land anymore.

It was about hearts.

And the men were ready to fight — Not with fists.

But with faith.

What It Takes to Live with Us

The ranchers kept coming.

One by one.

Sometimes two at a time.

Sometimes in groups.

They rode up confident, hats tipped low, boots polished. They brought gifts. Flowers tied with ribbon. Boxes of fine chocolates shipped in from the city. Silk scarves. Pretty shawls. Even dresses folded neatly in tissue paper.

They knew how to court.

That was the painful part.

Magnolia watched one man step down from his horse and present Millicent with a bouquet of red roses.

"For a lady who deserves beauty," he said.

Millicent didn't take them, but she didn't ignore him either. "You can leave them on the table," she said politely.

He smiled. "I'll come back tomorrow."

Marisol laughed later. "They smooth."

Moonland shook her head. "They studied women."

Margaret whispered. "They learned."

Miyako said quietly. "Our husbands never learned."

Marigold smirked. "They just stared."

Husbands Watch It All

From across the land, the husbands saw everything.

The gifts. The smiles. The bows. The flattery.

Paxton clenched his fists. "They embarrassing us."

Phoenix muttered. "They know how to talk."

Parker whispered. "They actually try."

Pierce swallowed. "I never bought her nothing."

Porter admitted, "I don't even know her favorite color."

Pablo whispered, "They courting my wife."

Preston stood still. "And we just watching."

The Question

That evening, the husbands finally came.

Not sneaking.

Not hiding.

They walked straight up to the porch where the women sat.

Magnolia looked up. "What do you need?"

Preston swallowed. "We want to live with you."

Silence.

Marisol crossed her arms. "Permanently?"

"Yes," Phoenix said. "As husbands."

Millicent raised an eyebrow. "Now you ready?"

Paxton nodded. "We are."

The Wives Speak Truth

Magnolia stood.

"You want to live with us..."

"But you never brought flowers."

Millicent added, "Never chocolates."

Marisol snapped, "Never a dress."

Moonland said quietly, "You only talk about physical affection."

Margaret added, "You don't court."

Miyako whispered, "You just watch."

Marigold finished, "And stare."

The men looked down.

Magnolia continued.

"These ranchers know how to court."

"They bring gifts."

"They write notes."

"They ask questions."

"They plan."

Marisol stepped forward.

"All you do is look."

"And hope."

Hard Truth

"You don't even know how to court a woman," Millicent said.

Paxton winced.

"Learn," Moonland added.

"From these other ranchers."

Phoenix looked up. "You want us to copy them?"

Magnolia shook her head.

"No."

"Learn the effort."

"The intention."

"The respect."

Marisol snapped, "Court us with your actions."

Men Broken

Parker's eyes filled. "We didn't know."

Marigold laughed softly. "You never asked."

Porter whispered, "We thought just being here was enough."

Magnolia replied, "It's not."

Silence fell.

The Challenge

Magnolia crossed her arms.

"If you want to live with us..."

"Court us."

"Properly."

Millicent smiled. "Win us."

Marisol smirked. "Like men."

Moonland said softly. "Like husbands."

Margaret nodded. "Not like prisoners."

Miyako added, "Not like watchers."

Marigold winked. "Surprise us."

Men Leave Changed

They walked away quietly.

No arguing.

No anger.

Paxton whispered, "They right."

Phoenix nodded. "We clueless."

Parker sighed. "We gotta learn."

Preston clenched his jaw. "I'm going to court my wife."

From the porch, Magnolia watched them walk away.

Millicent smiled. "They hurting."

Marisol shrugged. "They needed it."

Moonland whispered, "They'll grow."

Margaret nodded. "If they choose."

Miyako said softly, "God teaching."

Marigold laughed. "Let's see what they do."

Men awkwardly learning how to court • First flowers bought • First handwritten letters • Men asking for advice • Wives pretending not to notice

Chapter Eleven

Almost Losing Them**

The women did exactly what they said they would do.

They ignored them even more.

No smiling.

No soft words.

No lingering looks.

No accidental touches.

They walked past their husbands like strangers in town.

Not out of cruelty.

Out of purpose.

Magnolia whispered to the others, "We will not teach grown men how to love us."

Millicent nodded. "They need to want it bad."

Marisol said firmly, "Desperate bad."

Moonland added quietly, "Like they about to lose something precious."

Margaret whispered, "If we coach them, it won't be real."

Miyako agreed. "They must learn themselves."

Marigold smirked. "They need to feel this."

Men Feel the Distance

The husbands noticed immediately.

The space grew wider.

The silence deeper.

Preston watched Magnolia walk past without a glance.

His chest tightened.

"She really serious."

Paxton whispered, "She don't even look at me."

Phoenix swallowed. "I feel like I'm losing her."

Parker muttered, "I think we already lost them."

Pierce shook his head. "This hurts more than jail."

Porter sighed. "They not playing."

Pablo whispered, "I'm scared."

They Become Desperate

Paxton finally snapped. "I can't lose her."

Phoenix nodded. "Me neither."

Parker said, "I don't want another man taking my place."

Preston clenched his fists. "Then we fight... the right way."

Not with fists.

Not with pride.

With effort.

They Start Learning

The men did what the women told them.

They watched the ranchers.

How they tipped hats.

How they spoke gently.

How they brought gifts.

How they asked permission.

How they listened.

Phoenix said quietly, "They ask about her day."

Paxton nodded. "They remember details."

Parker added, "They show up with something in their hands."

Porter whispered, "They don't just stare."

Preston said, "They act."

First Attempts

Paxton rode into town awkwardly.

Bought:

Roses • Chocolates • A ribbon

He stood outside Marigold's ranch.

Heart pounding.

She walked past him.

Didn't stop.

Didn't look.

He whispered, "Marigold..."

She kept walking.

He stood there holding flowers like a fool.

Phoenix tried with Moonland.

Brought her a shawl.

She nodded politely.

"Thank you."

Walked away.

No smile.

Parker brought Millicent a small box.

Inside: earrings.

She took them.

"Appreciated."

No emotion.

Pierce tried to write a letter.

She read it.

Folded it.

Put it away.

Didn't respond.

Preston bought Magnolia a dress.

Left it on her porch.

She didn't bring it inside.

Just left it there.

For two days.

Men Feel the Pain

That night, the men gathered again.

Paxton stared at the ground. "She didn't even open the flowers."

Phoenix nodded. "She said thank you like I was a stranger."

Parker whispered, "I don't think it's enough."

Pierce said, "They making us earn it."

Porter sighed. "I deserve this."

Pablo whispered, "I feel like she slipping away."

Preston clenched his jaw. "Good."

They all looked at him.

"If we don't feel pain," he said, "we won't change."

Women Stand Firm

At the house, the women talked.

Millicent laughed softly. "They trying."

Marisol shrugged. "Too late?"

Moonland said, "Not yet."

Magnolia nodded. "They finally desperate."

Margaret whispered, "Good."

Miyako smiled. "They need to fear losing us."

Marigold grinned. "They should."

God in the Middle

Magnolia prayed quietly that night.

"Lord... break them."

"Not to destroy."

"But to rebuild."

Millicent whispered, "Let them learn."

Marisol added, "Not from us."

"But from You."

Men Pray Too

Preston knelt. "Lord... I'm scared."

Paxton cried. "I don't want to lose her."

Phoenix whispered, "Teach me."

Parker begged, "Help me love right."

Pierce said, "Change me."

Porter sighed, "I want to be worthy."

Pablo cried softly, "I choose her."

Pressure Builds

More ranchers came.

Better gifts.

Bigger promises.

One said to Magnolia, "I'll give you three hundred acres."

She replied calmly, "I'm married."

He smirked. "You don't live with him."

She stepped closer.

"I choose him."

And walked away.

The husbands saw.

And it shook them.

Paxton whispered, "She turned him down."

Phoenix nodded. "Even now."

Parker swallowed. "She loyal."

Preston said quietly, "Then we better become men worth being loyal to."

Silence.

Resolve.

When Men Finally Go to God**

They reached the end of themselves.

That was the truth.

No more plans. No more watching other men. No more guessing.

Paxton finally said it out loud.

"The only way we get our wives back... is through the Holy Spirit."

No one argued.

Phoenix nodded slowly. "We can't do this in our flesh."

Parker whispered, "We tried."

Pierce shook his head. "And failed."

Porter exhaled, "We don't know how to love them."

Pablo swallowed hard. "But God does."

Preston stood.

"Then we go to Him."

The Bible Opened

That night, the men sat in a circle.

No drinks. No jokes. No bravado.

Just Bibles.

Preston opened first.

"Ephesians 5:25," he read aloud.

'Husbands, love your wives, just as Christ loved the church and gave Himself up for her.'

Silence fell.

Paxton whispered, "He died for the church."

Phoenix nodded. "That's sacrifice."

Parker said quietly, "We never sacrificed."

Pierce swallowed. "We just wanted."

Porter whispered, "Selfish."

Pablo wiped his eyes. "We want to change."

Searching Scripture

They started flipping pages.

Colossians 3:19.

'Husbands, love your wives and do not be harsh with them.'

Phoenix closed his eyes.

"I been harsh."

Paxton nodded. "Me too."

Proverbs 31:11.

'Her husband trusts in her.'

Parker whispered, "We didn't trust them."

1 Peter 3:7.

'Husbands, live with your wives in an understanding way, showing honor.'

Pierce exhaled.

"We don't even understand them."

What Love Really Means

Preston spoke quietly.

"This ain't just physical."

"It's spiritual."

"Mental."

"Emotional."

"Physical comes last."

Paxton nodded.

"We been backwards."

Phoenix added, "We chased bodies."

Parker said, "But never learned hearts."

Porter whispered, "We want to know them."

They Admit Their Cravings

Paxton said it.

"I crave my wife."

Not lust.

Need.

Phoenix admitted, "I ache for her presence."

Parker whispered, "I just want to sit beside her."

Pierce said, "I want her to trust me."

Porter sighed, "I want her peace."

Pablo cried softly, "I want her laugh."

Preston closed his eyes.

"I need her."

Silence.

Men humbled.

Song of Solomon

Phoenix cleared his throat.

"I read this… and didn't understand it before."

He opened to Song of Solomon.

"My beloved is mine, and I am his."

Paxton swallowed.

"That's covenant."

Phoenix read on.

"You are altogether beautiful, my love; there is no flaw in you."

Parker whispered, "We never said that."

Pierce shook his head. "We thought it."

"But never spoke it," Porter added.

Phoenix continued.

"Set me as a seal upon your heart."

Pablo whispered, "That's loyalty."

They sat in awe.

"God wrote romance," Paxton said quietly.

"Not us."

Praying Differently

They dropped to their knees.

Not asking for bodies.

For change.

Preston prayed, "Lord... strip us."

Paxton cried, "Teach me to love."

Phoenix whispered, "Break my pride."

Parker begged, "Make me gentle."

Pierce said, "Make me patient."

Porter whispered, "Make me worthy."

Pablo sobbed, "I choose her."

The Realization

Preston lifted his head.

"We don't deserve them."

Phoenix nodded.

"But God gave us a chance."

Parker said, "Other men want them."

Paxton replied, "And they still ours."

Not possession.

Covenant.

Women at the Same Time

Across the land...

The women prayed too.

Magnolia whispered, "Lord... we feel their change."

Millicent nodded. "Keep us strong."

Marisol added, "Guard our hearts."

Moonland said softly, "If they change... we'll see it."

Margaret smiled. "Not hear it."

Miyako whispered, "Let it be real."

Marigold smirked. "Or we stay single wives."

They laughed.

The Men Decide

Preston stood.

"We not touching them."

Paxton nodded. "Not until invited."

Phoenix added, "We going to court right."

Parker said, "Not copy."

"Be real," Pierce added.

Porter whispered, "Daily."

Pablo nodded. "Consistent."

They closed their Bibles.

Different men.

Not perfect.

But broken.

And that's where God works best.

Preston whispered, "Only God can fix this."

Phoenix replied, "Then we stay in His face."

Paxton said, "Till they choose us."

Silence.

Hope.

What the Men Didn't Know

Was that the women wanted them too.

Not out of loneliness. Not out of fear. Not out of pressure.

But out of choice.

They just refused to settle for half-love.

They refused to accept men who only wanted their bodies. They refused to teach grown men how to value a woman. They refused to beg for flowers, for effort, for respect.

Magnolia said it plainly one night when the women were gathered:

"We want to be chosen the way Christ chose the church."

Millicent nodded. "With sacrifice."

Marisol added, "With intention."

Moonland said softly, "With protection."

Margaret whispered, "With patience."

Miyako smiled. "With understanding."

Marigold smirked. "With boldness."

They Wanted Spiritual Leadership

The women wanted men who would:

Pray without being asked • Read the Word on their own • Cover them spiritually • Lead with humility • Correct themselves before correcting a woman

Magnolia said, "We don't need preachers."

"We need men who obey God."

They Wanted Emotional Safety

Millicent admitted, "I want to talk without being dismissed."

Marisol said, "I want to be heard."

Moonland whispered, "I want peace, not control."

Margaret said, "I want consistency."

Miyako added, "I want gentleness."

Marigold laughed, "And some romance."

They Wanted Real Courtship

Not gifts for show. Not grand gestures for ego.

They wanted:

Handwritten letters • Remembered details • Thoughtful surprises • Time • Attention

Magnolia smiled, "Ask about my dreams."

"Not just my body."

They Wanted Protection, Not Possession

Marisol said, "Don't cage me."

"Cover me."

Moonland added, "Stand with me."

"Not over me."

Margaret whispered, "Defend my name."

Miyako said, "Even when I'm not there."

Marigold grinned, "Especially then."

They Wanted to Be Chosen Daily

Millicent said, "Marriage ain't a one-time vow."

"It's a daily decision."

Magnolia nodded, "Choose me every morning."

"Not because you have to."

"Because you want to."

The Silent Test

So they ignored them on purpose.

Not to punish.

To test.

Would the men:

Grow without being coached? • Seek God on their own? • Change when no one praised them? • Protect without touching? • Love without reward?

The women watched quietly.

From windows. From porches. From church pews.

And slowly...

They began to see something shift.

What They Started to Notice

Millicent whispered, "He prays now."

Marisol said, "Mine reads Scripture."

Moonland smiled, "He stopped staring."

297

Margaret added, "He listens."

Miyako said, "He serves."

Marigold laughed, "He nervous."

But They Stayed Guarded

Still...

They didn't soften.

Not yet.

Because love that lasts...

Shows itself over time.

Magnolia said, "One night don't change a man."

"Months do."

God in the Middle

And the men didn't know...

The women were praying too.

Not for comfort.

For confirmation.

"Lord," Magnolia whispered, "Show us if they're real."

Millicent added, "Not words."

"Fruit."

Marisol prayed, "Consistency."

Moonland said softly, "Truth."

Margaret whispered, "Growth."

Miyako added, "Humility."

Marigold smiled, "Romance too."

Closing Beat

Across the land...

Men praying. Women watching. God working.

Neither side knew the full story.

But heaven did.

Because both hearts...

Were being prepared.

Letters from the Heart

One evening, after much prayer, Magnolia spoke.

"We need to write."

The women looked up.

"To our husbands," she said. "Not to accuse."

"To explain."

Millicent nodded. "Tell them what we want."

Marisol added, "And ask them what they want."

Moonland whispered, "We're starting from nothing."

Margaret said softly, "A marriage born in court."

Miyako nodded. "Marry or be jailed."

Marigold sighed. "That's not romance."

They all laughed quietly.

"But it's our reality," Magnolia said.

"So we start fresh."

The Assignment

They wrote two things:

What they wanted from a husband • What they had been redeemed from

And they asked the men to do the same.

Not for arguments.

For understanding.

Magnolia's Letter

She wrote slowly.

Preston,

I want a man who prays without being asked. Who covers me spiritually. Who listens without correcting me. Who protects my name when I'm not around. Who courts me even after marriage.

I don't want perfection. I want consistency.

Now let me tell you something I never said out loud.

I was a high-class hostess. I served wealthy men. They paid for my company. But they never loved me.

I met Jesus Christ. He loved me without conditions. When I failed, He didn't leave.

Romans 8 says there is now no condemnation in Christ Jesus. That changed me.

I cannot give my body the way I once did. I am redeemed from that life. I would rather be alone than compromise.

Only the Holy Spirit taught me to love again. Even to love a husband I didn't choose at first.

If you want me, it must be for who I am now. Not for my body.

Magnolia

Millicent's Letter

Parker,

I want kindness. Patience. Protection.

I don't want control. I don't want ownership.

I was a hostess to powerful men. They used my presence. They never cared about my heart.

Jesus did.

He healed me. He restored me.

I learned that love doesn't demand. It gives.

I can't go back to being wanted only physically. I'm redeemed from that.

Millicent

Each Woman Confessed

Marisol wrote:

I will not be touched without honor. I was bought once. Never again.

Moonland wrote:

I choose holiness over loneliness.

Margaret wrote:

Jesus showed me what safe love feels like.

Miyako wrote:

I want peace in my home.

Marigold wrote:

I like romance — but I love righteousness.

Every letter ended the same way:

I was redeemed. I am not for sale. I will not be compromised.

They Waited

They sealed the letters.

Prayed.

Then sent word for the men to come collect them.

Men Receive Their Letters

Preston opened Magnolia's letter alone.

He read slowly.

Then stopped.

Then cried.

"She was never loved..."

He read again.

"Jesus loved her first."

He dropped to his knees.

"Lord... I never knew."

The Men Were Shaken

Paxton whispered, "They were hostesses?"

Phoenix nodded. "High class."

Parker swallowed, "They were used."

Pierce shook his head. "And still chose purity."

Porter whispered, "They chose God."

Pablo cried. "She trusted me with this."

Silence.

Heavy.

Holy.

The Men's Assignment

Preston said quietly, "We gotta write back."

Not excuses.

Not apologies.

Truth.

Why This Changed Everything

The men finally understood.

The women weren't withholding.

They were protecting their redemption.

They weren't cold.

They were healed.

They weren't testing.

They were guarding covenant.

Closing Beat

Magnolia sat by the window.

"They know now."

Millicent whispered, "Our truth."

Marisol smiled softly. "They see."

Moonland said, "Now the real test begins."

Margaret nodded. "Will they rise?"

Miyako whispered, "Or retreat."

Marigold grinned. "Let's see."

Chapter Twelve

Redeemed

The letters shook them.

There was no other word for it.

Each man sat alone with his wife's words, reading them again and again. Not skimming. Not rushing. But letting every sentence cut deep.

Paxton stared at Marigold's confession.

Phoenix reread Moonland's letter until the words blurred.

Parker pressed Millicent's pages to his chest.

Pierce sat on his bed, head in his hands.

Porter paced.

Pablo cried openly.

Preston didn't move at all.

They had known their wives were strong.

They had not known why.

The Hard Truth They Spoke Aloud

Paxton finally said what they were all thinking.

"I wanted a pure woman."

Silence.

"I wanted someone untouched."

Phoenix swallowed. "Me too."

Parker whispered, "I wanted a woman I could teach."

Pierce said quietly, "I wanted to be her first."

Porter admitted, "I wanted innocence."

Pablo nodded. "Someone I could brag about."

Preston exhaled slowly. "I wanted a woman who didn't have a past."

No one judged him.

Because they all felt it.

The Hypocrisy Exposed

Then Phoenix spoke.

"But we visited saloon girls."

Silence.

Paxton nodded. "More than once."

Parker whispered, "We had secret girlfriends."

Pierce said quietly, "Physical ones."

Porter clenched his jaw. "We did ungodly things."

Pablo bowed his head. "As rail police officers."

Preston said softly, "We weren't innocent."

They sat with that.

The weight of it.

The Revelation

Paxton finally said it.

"All sin is the same."

Phoenix nodded. "Pride."

"Lust."

"Anger."

"Hypocrisy."

Parker whispered, "We all fell short."

Pierce said, "Romans says that."

Porter nodded. "All have sinned."

Pablo added, "Only Jesus was without sin."

Preston closed his eyes.

"And we judged them."

Silence fell heavy.

The Woman Caught in Adultery

Phoenix opened his Bible.

John 8.

He read aloud.

"Let him who is without sin cast the first stone."

Paxton whispered, "And they all walked away."

Parker said, "Because none of them were innocent."

Pierce nodded. "And neither are we."

Porter swallowed. "We were ready to stone our wives."

Pablo whispered, "But we sinners too."

Preston spoke firmly.

"We drop the stones."

Redemption

Paxton's voice broke.

"They found Jesus."

Phoenix nodded. "And He loved them."

Parker said, "Unconditionally."

Pierce added, "When they failed."

Porter whispered, "He didn't condemn."

Pablo cried. "And neither should we."

Preston clenched his fists.

"We found redemption too."

Silence.

Holy silence.

What They Wrote

That night, they wrote back.

Not defensively.

Not prideful.

Repentant.

Preston's Letter

Magnolia,

Reading your letter hurt. Not because of your past. But because I judged you.

I wanted a pure woman. But I wasn't pure.

I sinned. I visited women. I lived wrong.

I have no stones to throw.

Jesus forgave me. So I forgive and honor you.

We are both redeemed. That's how I want to start our marriage.

Not as judge and accused. But as two forgiven people.

Preston

The Others Wrote the Same Truth

Paxton wrote:

I wanted innocence. But I was not innocent.
We are equal sinners. Equal in grace.

Phoenix wrote:

Your past does not scare me. Your redemption
inspires me.

Parker wrote:

I will never hold your past over you. Because
Christ didn't hold mine.

Pierce wrote:

I choose you. Not your history.

Porter wrote:

We start new. Together.

Pablo wrote:

We are redeemed. That is enough.

The New Beginning

When the women read the letters...

They cried.

Not tears of fear.

Tears of relief.

Magnolia whispered, "He understands."

Millicent smiled. "He repented."

Marisol nodded. "He didn't judge."

Moonland closed her eyes. "He chose grace."

Margaret whispered, "We're free."

Miyako smiled. "This is real."

Marigold laughed softly. "They finally grew up."

Magnolia lifted her hands.

"Thank You, Jesus."

Millicent whispered, "For redemption."

Marisol added, "For second chances."

Moonland said, "For real love."

Margaret smiled. "For grace."

Miyako nodded. "For mercy."

Marigold grinned. "For new beginnings."

315

Final Beat

Across the land...

Seven men prayed.

Seven women wept.

Heaven smiled.

Because this marriage...

Was no longer about the past.

It was about redemption.

Home at Last

The next week came softly.

Not with drama. Not with fanfare.

But with decision.

Seven wagons rolled up the long drive to the new ranch house.

Seven men stepped down.

No hesitation. No second thoughts. No fear.

They weren't visiting.

They were moving in.

Permanently.

Preston stood beside Magnolia, hat in his hands.

"I'm home," he said quietly.

Her eyes softened.

"So am I."

One by one, the other men spoke the same words.

Paxton to Marigold. Phoenix to Moonland. Parker to Millicent. Pierce to Miyako. Porter to Margaret. Pablo to Marisol.

"I'm not leaving."

Not as a threat. As a promise.

The women watched them unload.

Trunks. Books. Clothes. Tools.

Not much.

But enough.

Magnolia whispered to Millicent, "They serious."

Millicent smiled. "They chose us."

Marisol nodded. "For real."

Settling In

Rooms were claimed.

Shoes placed by doors.

Hats hung on hooks.

The house felt... different.

Full.

Alive.

Safe.

That evening, they ate together.

Not a feast.

Simple food.

Laughter.

Stories.

The men listened more than they spoke.

Magnolia noticed.

Night Comes

When the lamps were dimmed...

Each couple moved quietly to their rooms.

Not rushed.

Not nervous.

But intentional.

Preston stood in Magnolia's doorway.

"Before anything," he said, "can we pray?"

She smiled.

"Yes."

They held hands.

"Lord," Preston whispered, "thank You for redemption."

"For second chances."

"For this woman."

Magnolia prayed too.

"Cover our marriage."

"Keep it holy."

"Let love lead."

They said amen.

Consummation with Honor

They didn't rush.

No pressure. No performance.

Just:

eye contact • soft words • gentle hands • trust

Not from lust.

From covenant.

From choice.

From healing.

The same thing happened in every room.

Paxton cried before touching Marigold.

"I waited," he said.

"And I chose you."

Phoenix held Moonland's face.

"Not because I have to."

"Because I want to."

Parker whispered to Millicent,

"You're my only."

Pierce told Miyako,

"I'm grateful."

Porter said to Margaret,

"This is sacred."

Pablo told Marisol,

"You are safe."

No shame.

No past.

Just present.

Morning Light

Sunlight filled the halls.

Men stretched.

Women laughed.

Breakfast smells drifted.

No awkwardness.

No fear.

Just peace.

Paxton whispered, "I slept good."

Marigold smirked. "Me too."

Phoenix smiled softly.

"I ain't going nowhere."

Moonland replied, "Good."

Permanent

They sat at the long table together.

Seven couples.

No separation now.

Magnolia looked at Preston.

"You staying?"

He squeezed her hand.

"For life."

Millicent smiled at Parker.

"You chose me."

He nodded.

"Every day."

Marisol laughed.

"This is it."

Moonland said softly, "Covenant."

Margaret whispered, "Redeemed."

Miyako smiled.

"New beginnings."

Marigold grinned.

"Told y'all."

They laughed.

Outside, the land stretched wide.

Inside, love grew deeper.

Not perfect.

But real.

They didn't come together out of force.

And heaven smiled.

Because this marriage...

Was built on redemption.

Chapter Thirteen

The Women They Left Behind

Several months before the men ever left the force...

Before ranch land. Before court marriages. Before redemption.

They were stationed in a small town in Oklahoma.

A dusty place. Quiet. But dangerous.

They were on stakeout duty.

A gang had been robbing trains. Stealing payroll money. Hitting hard and disappearing fast.

Word was...

After every robbery, the gang hid out in this town.

So the seven rangers were sent in.

Watching. Waiting. Blending in.

They were not married then.

They were young. Strong. Lonely.

And that's when they met seven women.

The Teachers

The women had just arrived in town.

They were educated. Well-spoken. Proper.

They came to start a school for children.

Poor children. Railroad children. Orphans.

They had hearts for community.

Passion.

Vision.

They wore long dresses. High collars. Hair neatly pinned.

They were not flashy.

But beautiful.

The kind of beauty that came from purpose.

Their Conversations

The rangers and the teachers met often.

At the general store. Outside the schoolhouse. At community gatherings.

They talked for hours.

About:

books • faith • children • dreams • land • building communities

The women admired the men.

Strong. Protective. Honorable.

The men admired the women.

Pure. Soft-spoken. Devoted.

Without realizing it...

The women fell in love.

They didn't say it.

But they felt it.

Each of them.

They watched how the men treated people.

How they protected children.

How they stood guard all night.

They imagined futures.

Families. Homes. Church together.

The Men's Offer

One evening, after a long shift...

Paxton had said,

"When we build our ranch..."

"You ladies should come visit."

Phoenix nodded.

"See if you like it."

Parker added,

"Maybe start a bigger school."

They smiled.

"Maybe," they said.

No marriage promises.

No engagements.

Just...

Hope.

The Transfer

Not long after...

Orders came in.

The men were being transferred.

New assignment.

New territory.

They met the teachers one last time.

Told them the town they were homesteading.

Gave them the address.

Again...

No marriage promises.

Just:

"Come visit someday."

The men left.

The women waved.

Heartbroken.

But hopeful.

The Teachers' Assumptions

The women gathered that night.

They cried.

But they believed something else.

"This is a prelude to marriage," Lydia said.

"They wouldn't invite us if they weren't serious," Lillian added.

Lucinda whispered,

"They working to build a home for us."

They agreed.

They did not date anyone else.

They stayed faithful.

They believed they were:

decent • modest • godly

Perfect wives.

Their Names

They named themselves one night for fun.

All first names starting with L Last name Teacher.

Lydia Teacher • Lillian Teacher • Lucinda Teacher • Louisa Teacher • Loretta Teacher • Leona Teacher • Lavender Teacher

The Big Decision

After months passed...

They made a choice.

They would not renew their school term.

They would go together.

To visit the rangers.

To see their ranch.

They believed:

The men were building homes for them.

They believed:

Marriage was coming.

Their Plans

They packed carefully.

Beautiful day dresses. Soft night gowns.
Church outfits.

Each woman packed:

a simple wedding dress • gloves • veils • small
accessories

Just in case.

They saved enough money:

To stay in a boardinghouse for two months.

They believed:

That would be plenty of time for wedding
plans.

Their Faith

They were raised strict.

Church every Sunday. Bible every morning.

No touching. No kissing.

Until marriage.

They believed the men expected the same.

The Surprise

The men had not written yet.

But the women decided:

"We will surprise them."

They bought second-class tickets.

Cheap. Crowded. Exciting.

They didn't care.

They were in love.

On the Train

The train rattled.

Smoke filled the air.

They sat together.

Laughing. Dreaming.

"What will his house look like?" "Will he ask me right away?" "Will there be a church?" "How many children?"

They planned everything.

Their Expectations

They knew:

It might take time.

Men need money.

Land takes work.

They were willing to wait.

They would:

Stay in a boardinghouse. Pay week to week. Help however they could.

They were patient women.

They Felt Safe

Because they had each other.

Like sisters.

They traveled together. Worked together. Prayed together.

They trusted God.

They trusted the men.

As the train moved forward...

Seven hopeful women looked out the windows.

They believed:

They were going to meet their future husbands.

They had no idea...

Everything had changed.

The Arrival

The train finally hissed to a stop.

Steam clouded the platform.

Seven women stepped down together, skirts neat, gloves on, hats straight.

Lydia Teacher looked around first. "This is it."

Lillian Teacher pressed her hands together. "My heart is beating so fast."

Lucinda Teacher whispered, "We're really here."

They gathered their bags and walked toward the boardinghouse.

Checking In

The landlady eyed them.

"Seven rooms?"

"Yes, ma'am," Loretta said politely.

"For how long?"

"Week to week," Lavender answered. "We're waiting on... friends."

The woman slid the register forward.

"Sign here."

Pens scratched.

Keys were handed out.

Rooms assigned.

They climbed the stairs quietly, reverent almost.

That Night

They unpacked.

Laid out dresses.

Straightened veils.

Leona whispered, "What if they ask us right away?"

Lydia smiled. "I brought my white dress."

They knelt by their beds and prayed.

"Lord," Lucinda whispered, "we trust You."

They slept restless.

Saturday Morning

They rose early.

Dressed trim and proper.

High collars. Pressed skirts. Hair pinned neat.

They rented three wagons.

They drove the wagons, three of them.

At the Old Ranch

They stopped at the first ranch.

Wood warped. Roof sagging. Windows cracked.

"This must be it," Loretta whispered.

They stepped inside.

Dust. Rough furniture.

But something felt wrong.

Lucinda frowned. "There's no clothing."

Leona opened a drawer. "Empty."

"Someone moved out," Lavender said slowly.

"But why leave everything else?"

They looked around.

"We can help them," Lillian said. "Fix it up."

Waiting

They sat on the porch.

Hours passed.

No men.

339

They had brought food from the boardinghouse.

"We'll make supper," Lydia said.

They lit a fire.

Smoke rose up the chimney.

They waited.

Still nothing.

The New House

Just before dusk, Loretta pointed.

"Look."

Not far away...

A beautiful house.

Fresh wood. Tall windows. White trim.

"Who lives there?" Lucinda asked the driver.

He frowned. "Some folks. Married couples."

They exchanged glances.

"Married?" Lydia whispered.

The Walk

They loaded the food back into the wagons.

"This must be where they are," Lillian said.

They approached.

Lights glowed inside.

Voices.

Laughter.

The Knock

Lavender knocked.

A woman opened the door.

Magnolia.

"Yes?"

Lydia smiled nervously.

"We're looking for seven men."

Magnolia blinked.

"Come in," she said calmly. "We're eating."

Inside

They stepped in.

And froze.

Seven men.

Laughing.

Arms around women.

Their men.

Lydia gasped.

"What... is this?"

Lucinda whispered, "Who are these women?"

Silence.

The men stood up.

Preston stammered, "What are you doing here?"

Loretta screamed, "Who are THESE women?!"

Preston swallowed.

"These... are our wives."

Explosion

Lydia screamed.

"LIAR!"

Plates flew.

Food splattered walls.

"You CHEATED!"

"You TRAITOR!"

"You INFIDEL!"

Lavender hurled bread.

"You made us wait!"

Lucinda sobbed.

"We saved ourselves for you!"

Leona screamed.

"We thought you were building a home FOR US!"

Chaos

The teachers attacked.

Punching.

343

Kicking.

Slapping.

"You used us!"

"You lied!"

"You disgust us!"

The men tried to calm them.

"Please—"

"Stop—"

"Listen—"

They were shoved.

Kicked.

Hit.

The Wives

The wives said nothing.

They just...

cleaned.

Marigold laughed softly.

"They getting beat again."

Millicent wiped gravy off the wall.

Magnolia shook her head smiling.

Outside

The teachers followed them out.

Throwing dirt.

Sticks.

Stones.

"You ruined our lives!"

"We waited for you!"

"Divorce them!"

"DIVORCE THEM!"

Lydia screamed.

345

"We demand it!"

The men shouted back.

"We will explain TOMORROW!"

They put the women in wagons.

"Go back to town!"

"We'll come talk!"

The teachers cried.

"This is a mistake!"

Back Inside

The men came back.

Bruised.

Dirty.

Ashamed.

Their wives were seated.

Plates remade.

Food waiting.

Magnolia laughed.

"Women beat you again?"

Marisol smirked.

"You attract trouble."

The Explanation

Preston sighed.

"They were teachers in Oklahoma."

Phoenix added, "They started a school."

Paxton said, "They thought we were going to marry them."

"But we never promised," Parker said.

"Never kissed them," Pierce added.

Porter shook his head.

"They misunderstood."

The Wives Go Quiet

"What do they want?" Magnolia asked.

Preston whispered.

"They want us to divorce you."

Silence.

You could hear breathing.

Marigold slowly stood.

"Divorce?"

Magnolia's eyes went cold.

Millicent whispered Scripture:

"What God has joined together, let no man separate." – Mark 10:9

Marisol folded her arms.

"They want to break covenant?"

Moonland whispered.

"After all we've been through?"

Margaret stood slowly.

"Tell them…"

Miyako finished.

"No."

Marigold smiled darkly.

"They'll learn."

Magnolia looked at Preston.

"You staying?"

"For life," he said.

She nodded.

"Then they will scream."

The Sheriff's Office

The seven teachers drove the wagons.

No drivers.

No help.

Just trembling hands on reins and swollen eyes.

Lydia Teacher wiped her face with her glove. "They humiliated us."

Lillian sobbed. "They hugged those women in front of us."

Lucinda shook. "We waited. We stayed pure."

Loretta clenched her fists. "They betrayed us."

Leona whispered, "I feel used."

Lavender cried, "They promised us hope."

They turned the wagons toward the sheriff's office instead of the boardinghouse.

Not to rest.

To fight.

Inside the Sheriff's Office

The sheriff looked up when the door burst open.

Seven women.

Tears. Shaking. Anger.

"What's wrong, ladies?" he asked calmly.

Lydia slammed her hand on the counter.

"We want justice!"

Lucinda cried, "We demand a petition!"

"For what?" he asked.

"FOR DIVORCE," Loretta shouted. "And immediate marriage to us!"

The sheriff blinked.

"Whose divorce?"

"Seven men," Leona said. "The ex-rail officers!"

Lavender screamed, "They MANHANDLED us!"

"They dragged us outside!"

"They embarrassed us!"

"They owe us!"

The Sheriff's Response

He leaned back slowly.

"Now hold on."

"It's late."

"Courts closed."

"If you feel you were physically harmed, you can file a summons in the morning."

Lydia wiped her face.

"So we come back tomorrow?"

"Yes ma'am."

"We want them arrested," Lillian said. "Until we see the judge!"

He shook his head.

"I can't do that tonight."

Lucinda sobbed, "They destroyed our futures!"

Private Thoughts

The sheriff didn't say it out loud.

But inside he thought:

Them boys in trouble again.

He leaned back.

"Who exactly?"

"The seven ex-rail men," Lydia said firmly.

He didn't mention their wives.

Didn't mention the forced marriages.

But inside...

Oh boy.

This town about to light up again.

Drama Builds

They cried.

They ranted.

They paced.

"They cheated!" "They LIED!" "They should be punished!" "They used us!"

The sheriff finally said gently,

"Go get some rest."

"Come back in the morning."

"We'll handle this proper."

Outside

They stumbled out.

Collapsed into their wagons.

Loretta sobbed, "I thought he loved me."

Leona cried, "I saved myself for him."

Lavender whispered, "How could he?"

Lucinda shook.

"They replaced us."

Lydia wiped her face.

"We are NOT done."

The Sheriff Alone

He locked up.

Looked out the window.

"This town," he muttered.

"Always something."

He shook his head.

"Tomorrow gonna be somethin'."

He could already see it:

Court drama • Town gossip • Newspaper headlines • Women yelling • Men defending • Wives standing firm

He sighed.

"Lord help me."

The moon hung low.

Seven broken women rode back to town.

Seven married women sat in a warm house.

Seven men lay uneasy in their beds.

The Morning After

Before sunrise, the seven husbands gathered in the barn.

Preston Protect Paxton Protect Phoenix Protect Parker Protect Pierce Protect Porter Protect Pablo Protect

They stood in a circle, hats off, heads bowed.

Preston prayed first. "Lord, you see this mess. We need Your wisdom. Guard our wives. Guard our words."

Paxton added, "Give us truth without cruelty."

Phoenix whispered, "Help us stand firm."

Parker said, "Keep us from fear."

Pierce prayed, "Cover our marriages."

Porter asked, "Protect our homes."

Pablo finished, "Let Your will be done."

Amen echoed softly.

With Their Wives

They kissed their wives' foreheads.

Not passionate. Protective.

"If we're not back by evening," Preston told Magnolia, "go see the sheriff."

Magnolia nodded. "We trust God."

Marisol said to Pablo, "Don't fight."

Moonland whispered to Phoenix, "Speak truth."

Millicent squeezed Parker's hand. "Stand firm."

Margaret smiled at Porter. "We praying."

Miyako hugged Pierce. "Be gentle."

Marigold smirked at Paxton. "Don't let them run you."

The women stayed behind.

They knew heartbreak. They knew disappointment.

They had lived it.

They prayed for the teachers.

And for their husbands.

At the Boardinghouse

The men walked into the parlor.

The proprietor peeked from behind her desk.

Lord have mercy, she muttered. These boys in trouble again.

Seven teachers sat stiffly.

Eyes swollen. Faces red.

Lydia Teacher Lillian Teacher Lucinda Teacher Louisa Teacher Loretta Teacher Leona Teacher Lavender Teacher

Lydia stood first.

"So you finally came."

Paxton swallowed. "We said we would."

Lucinda snapped, "Why are you here?"

Preston answered carefully, "To clear misunderstandings."

The Accusations

"You LIED," Loretta shouted. "You made us believe!"

Phoenix raised his hands. "We never promised marriage."

Leona cried, "You implied a relationship!"

Parker shook his head. "We never said we loved you."

"You asked us to visit!" Lavender yelled.

Pierce sighed. "Come see the ranch. That's all."

Louisa sobbed, "We thought it was a proposal!"

"We brought dresses!" Lydia screamed. "Wedding dresses!"

Porter whispered, "We didn't know."

Threats

"You will divorce those women," Lillian demanded. "And marry us immediately."

Pablo stood firm. "No."

The room went silent.

Lucinda hissed, "Then we'll file charges."

"Breach of promise!"

"And assault!" Leona shouted. "You tried to force us into wagons!"

Paxton snapped, "You were throwing rocks!"

Phoenix added, "We were defending ourselves!"

The Truth Comes Out

Preston took a breath.

"The judge gave us a choice."

"Three years in jail..."

"Or marriage."

"We chose marriage."

Lavender gasped. "You could have waited!"

Lydia cried, "Three years is nothing!"

Paxton shook his head. "We're not divorcing."

Porter added, "Our wives are our covenant."

Parker said, "We chose them."

The Teachers' Rage

"You TRAITORS!"

"You used us!"

"You wasted our youth!"

Lucinda collapsed into a chair sobbing.

"We trusted you."

Lydia wiped her face angrily. "You'll regret this."

"We're seeing the judge," Loretta snapped. "Today."

Leona pointed. "You WILL hear from us."

Final Stand

Preston stepped forward.

"We are not leaving our wives."

Phoenix nodded. "We'll face whatever comes."

Paxton added, "But we will not sin to fix a misunderstanding."

Porter whispered, "We ask for forgiveness"

361

Pablo said softly, "But we choose to keep our marriages."

The teachers stormed out the parlor.

Crying.

Shouting.

Threatening.

The proprietor shook her head.

"Y'all sure know how to stir things up."

Preston sighed. "Seems like it."

Outside, the men stood silent.

Paxton whispered, "They serious."

Phoenix replied, "So are we."

Preston straightened.

"Let's go home."

Chapter Fourteen

The Courtroom Erupts

The seven teachers marched straight to the sheriff's office.

No hesitation.

No fear.

They were still shaken from the night before.

Eyes red. Voices sharp. Hearts wounded.

Lydia Teacher spoke first.

"We are here to file a formal complaint."

The sheriff looked up slowly.

"Against the Protects?"

"Yes the seven ex-rail men," Lillian Teacher said.

Lucinda stepped forward.

"They deceived us."

Loretta added.

"They humiliated us."

Leona snapped.

"They physically forced us into wagons last night."

Lavender cried.

"They owe us justice."

Their Complaint

They spoke over one another.

"You implied marriage!" "You invited us!" "We saved ourselves!" "We brought wedding dresses!" "You dragged us!" "You embarrassed us in front of their wives!"

The sheriff wrote quietly.

Didn't interrupt.

Didn't react.

Just listened.

When they finished, Lydia slammed her hand on the desk.

"We demand they divorce those women and marry us."

Silence.

The sheriff leaned back.

"I'll take this to the judge."

The Protectors Stay in Town

Across the street, the seven husbands waited.

Preston Protect Paxton Protect Phoenix
Protect Parker Protect Pierce Protect Porter
Protect Pablo Protect

They sent word to the sheriff.

If you need us, we're still here.

They weren't running.

They weren't hiding.

They were standing.

The Judge Reads the Complaint

The sheriff walked into the judge's chambers.

Handed him the papers.

The judge read slowly.

Brows lifting.

Then lowering.

He sighed.

"This again, the same seven men?"

He shook his head.

"Set court."

"I want everyone present."

"Teachers."

"Protectors."

"And their wives."

Summoning the Wives

Preston volunteered.

"I'll go."

He rode fast.

Pulled up to the ranch.

"Maggie," he called.

"Court."

Magnolia nodded.

"We'll be there."

The other wives gathered.

Millicent. Marisol. Moonland. Margaret. Miyako. Marigold.

No fear.

They dressed modest.

Hats on.

Spines straight.

Courtroom Packed

By afternoon...

The courtroom was overflowing.

Town folks.

Shop owners.

Rail workers.

Farmers.

Newspaper reporters with notebooks ready.

Whispers everywhere.

"This about the forced marriages."

"No, it's about those teachers."

"They want them men."

The gavel slammed.

"Court is now in session."

Teachers Speak

Lydia stood.

Voice shaking.

"We were deceived."

Lillian added.

"They invited us."

Lucinda cried.

"We thought marriage was coming."

Loretta snapped.

"We brought dresses."

Leona pointed at the men.

"They manhandled us."

Lavender sobbed.

"They embarrassed us."

"They owe us."

"They MUST divorce."

Protectors Respond

Preston stood.

"Your honor..."

"We never promised marriage."

Paxton added.

"We never kissed them."

369

Phoenix said.

"We never said we loved them."

Parker spoke.

"We invited them to visit."

Pierce said.

"Nothing more."

Porter continued.

"We defended ourselves when they attacked us."

Pablo finished.

"We were married by your order."

Judge Questions

The judge leaned forward.

"Teachers..."

"What do you want?"

Lydia spoke boldly.

"Divorce."

"Immediately."

"And marriage to us."

Gasps filled the room.

The Protectors' Stand

Preston spoke firmly.

"Your honor…"

"You ordered us to marry."

"We consented."

"We chose our wives."

"We will not divorce."

Paxton added.

"We stand by our covenant."

Phoenix said.

"We are not leaving."

Parker nodded.

"This is final."

The Court Reacts

Whispers.

Murmurs.

Shock.

The wives sat silent.

Heads held high.

Marigold smirked.

"They bold."

Magnolia whispered.

"Watch God."

Judge Speaks

The judge raised his hand.

"Silence."

"You are asking me to break a marriage I ordered."

"That is serious."

He looked at the teachers.

"You assumed marriage."

"But assumptions aren't contracts."

He looked at the men.

"You consented."

"You chose."

"This court does NOT undo covenants."

The teachers gasped.

The wives squeezed hands.

The men stood firm.

Reporters scribbled furiously.

This wasn't over.

But the line had been drawn.

Public Exposure**

The judge lifted his hand again.

"Silence in this courtroom."

The murmurs faded, but the air stayed thick.

He turned to the teachers.

"I have heard your complaint."

"You assumed marriage."

"You were never promised marriage."

"You traveled on your own decision."

Lydia shot back, "We left our JOBS!"

"We gave up everything!"

Lucinda cried, "Our school!"

"Our children!"

"Our lives!"

Loretta snapped, "They ruined us!"

The judge nodded slowly.

"I hear that."

Then he looked at the Protectors.

"You will reimburse these women for their travel expenses."

Gasps rippled through the courtroom.

The men nodded immediately.

"Yes, sir," Preston said. "We will."

Paxton added, "That's fair."

Teachers Push Harder

"But that's not enough!" Lydia shouted.

"We don't want money!"

"We want THEM!"

She pointed wildly.

"Divorce those women!"

"Marry us!"

"NOW!"

The courtroom erupted.

Reporters leaned forward.

Pens flew.

Judge's Question

The judge leaned back.

"Let me ask you something."

"Do you truly believe..."

"Those men would LOVE you?"

Silence.

Then Lillian said firmly, "We can make them love us."

Lucinda nodded. "In time."

Loretta smirked, "Men learn."

Leona added, "They'll forget."

The courtroom burst into laughter.

Men chuckled.

Women gasped.

Someone whispered, "That ain't love."

The judge banged his gavel.

"Order!"

But even he smiled slightly.

Public Reaction

A farmer muttered, "Make him love you?"

Another said, "That ain't marriage."

Someone laughed loudly, "Sounds like jail again!"

Reporters scribbled furiously.

This was gold.

Teachers Meltdown

Lavender screamed, "You're all heartless!"

"They USED us!"

Lydia sobbed, "They OWE us!"

Lucinda pointed at the wives'.

"They STOLE them!"

The judge cut her off.

"Enough."

Judge's Ruling

"This court will not force love."

"This court will not dissolve marriages based on assumptions."

"You will receive compensation for travel."

"That is all."

He slammed the gavel.

"Court adjourned."

Aftermath – Same Day

The teachers stormed out.

Crying.

Yelling.

Threatening reporters.

"You print lies!"

"We were betrayed!"

Outside...

Town folks buzzed.

"I can't believe they thought that."

"Trying to force love."

"Shameful."

"Their poor hearts."

"They lost everything."

"But still wrong."

The Protectors stood stiff.

Preston whispered, "That was brutal."

Paxton sighed, "They humiliated themselves."

Phoenix shook his head. "Love can't be forced."

Parker added, "God did this."

Judge to Himself

The judge sat back.

"This town..."

"Never boring."

He sighed.

"Lord help us."

The wives walked out first.

Heads high.

Silent.

Strong.

The men followed.

The teachers collapsed on the courthouse steps.

Sobbing.

Broken.

Reporters circled.

And by sundown...

The whole town knew.

Taking It Higher

The teachers gathered themselves on the courthouse steps.

Tears still streaked their faces, but now their posture changed.

This was no longer grief.

This was determination.

Lydia straightened her hat. "We are not leaving this town."

Lucinda wiped her cheeks. "And we are not letting this die here."

Loretta nodded. "We are taking this higher."

Lavender whispered, "To a higher judge."

Leona lifted her chin. "A federal one."

Their New Plan

Lydia spoke firmly to the reporters.

"If one judge had the power to order men to marry…"

"Then another judge has the power to order a divorce."

Gasps rippled.

"This court forced a marriage," Lucinda said. "So now we demand the same power be used to free them."

Loretta added sharply, "Justice works both ways."

"We want a federal judge to hear this case."

"Not a small-town courtroom."

Their Demand

"We want divorce," Lydia declared.

"Court-ordered."

"And then," Lucinda said coldly, "marriage to us."

The crowd murmured.

Lavender added, "They can learn to love us."

Leona nodded. "We will make them fall in love."

Silence fell.

Press Frenzy

Reporters pushed closer.

"Are you saying you want the government to force love?"

Lydia snapped back, "No."

"But they already forced marriage."

"This is about equal power."

Lucinda added, "If the law can bind..."

"It can unbind."

Pens flew across paper.

Headlines were forming.

Religious Supporters

Several church women stood nearby.

"We support your right to justice," one said.

"You were misled."

Another added, "Take it higher."

"Don't let them silence you."

The teachers nodded.

The Wives Remain Silent

Across the street...

The wives stood together.

Not one word.

No defense.

No insults.

No tears.

Magnolia folded her hands.

Millicent stared forward.

Marisol breathed slow.

Moonland whispered a prayer.

Margaret stood still.

Miyako lowered her eyes.

Marigold crossed her arms.

Silent strength.

Town Reaction

People whispered:

"They really going federal?"

"That's serious."

"Can a judge force divorce?"

"This story just got bigger."

The sheriff muttered under his breath, "This town about to be famous."

The Teachers' Vow

Lydia raised her voice.

"We will not stop."

"We will petition higher courts."

"We will make this a national issue."

Lucinda added, "They don't get to walk away."

Loretta said, "We are not ashamed."

Lavender whispered, "We believed in love."

Leona finished, "And we still do."

The courthouse steps buzzed.

Reporters scribbled.

Townfolk whispered.

Wives silent.

Husbands tense.

And seven women stood firm in their vow:

They would not accept defeat.

They would escalate.

Taking It All the Way

The teachers had no idea what the law really required.

They thought they could simply appeal to a "higher judge."

But when one reporter explained quietly,

"You can only appeal that ruling to the Supreme Court,"

they froze.

Lydia blinked. "The Supreme Court?"

The reporter nodded. "That's the next level."

Lucinda whispered, "So we can't just go to another courthouse?"

"No," he said. "You either file the paperwork yourselves or hire an attorney."

Their Decision

The women gathered in a tight circle.

"We don't have money for a lawyer," Loretta said.

Leona shook her head. "Not after quitting our jobs."

Lavender lifted her chin. "We'll do it ourselves."

Lucinda nodded. "Pro se."

"Just us."

They clasped hands.

"We've been educated women," Lydia said. "We can write."

"We can argue."

"We can fight."

Their Legal Strategy

They began drafting their appeal that very evening.

Their claim:

The lower judge used undue pressure • The punishment did not match the crime • Three years in jail or forced marriage was overbearing and unjust • The sentence was coercive • The marriages were entered under duress

Lydia read aloud what she wrote:

"This court imposed a punishment that exceeded the alleged offense. The defendants were pressured into marriage under threat of imprisonment."

Lucinda added,

"The law should not force permanent union as punishment."

Loretta said,

"This sentence deprived the men of free choice."

Their Accusation

Leona hesitated, then said,

"He did it because he felt sorry for those wives."

"They needed protection too," Lavender added.

"We needed protection also," Lydia said firmly.

"We were vulnerable."

"We left our jobs."

"We trusted those men."

Lucinda slammed her pen down.

"He chose sides."

Their Demand

They wrote their conclusion clearly:

"We request this court overturn the sentence."

"We request court-ordered divorce."

"And due to implied relationship," Loretta added,

"we request marriage to the defendants."

Lavender whispered,

"We will make them fall in love with us."

Leona nodded.

"In time."

Town Reaction

People overheard them at the boardinghouse.

"She's serious." "They filing Supreme Court?" "Lord help this town." "That's bold."

The proprietor shook her head.

"These girls don't quit."

The Men Hear

Word reached the Protectors.

Phoenix muttered, "They going all the way."

Paxton shook his head. "They serious."

Preston said quietly,

"Let them."

"Our marriage stands."

The Wives Remain Silent

The wives heard too.

Still said nothing.

Magnolia folded laundry.

Millicent watered plants.

Marisol swept the porch.

Moonland prayed.

Margaret baked.

Miyako sewed.

Marigold smiled to herself.

Their silence was not weakness.

It was confidence.

Seven women sat around a table covered in papers.

Pens scratching.

Eyes burning.

Determined.

They believed:

Law would fix what love did not.

But they didn't know...

Some things cannot be forced.

Not marriage.

Not loyalty.

Not hearts.

Chapter Fifteen

Thirty Days to Change Everything

The teachers were given thirty days to file their appeal.

They did it in one week.

No sleep. No rest. No hesitation.

They sat around a long table in the boardinghouse parlor.

Papers everywhere. Ink stains. Red eyes. Tired hands.

But fierce.

Their Filing

Lydia read aloud what they had written.

"This appeal challenges the lower court's ruling on grounds of undue pressure and judicial overreach."

Lucinda added,

"The judge forced these men into marriage under threat of incarceration."

Loretta leaned forward.

Three years in jail for a public disturbance is excessive."

"Overbearing."

"Unjust."

Leona slammed her palm on the table.

"He used punishment to force a lifelong decision!"

Lavender wrote quickly.

"This violates basic human liberty."

Their Claim

They stated clearly:

The punishment did not fit the crime • The judge used fear to coerce marriage • The men did not freely choose • The court abused authority • The marriages were entered under duress

Lydia read:

"These unions were not born from love or intent, but from judicial threat."

Their Hurt

Lucinda wiped her face.

"We suffered harm."

"We left our jobs."

"Our school."

"Our purpose."

Loretta said bitterly,

"We believed them."

"We waited."

"We planned weddings."

Lavender whispered,

"They replaced us."

Leona nodded.

"Our pain deserves retribution."

Their Demand for Protection

"They gave those wives protection," Lydia said.

"But we needed protection too."

Lucinda added,

"We were vulnerable."

"We traveled alone."

"We were humiliated publicly."

Loretta snapped,

"He chose sides."

"They didn't deserve special treatment."

Their Requests

They wrote their demands boldly:

Overturn the sentence • Declare the marriages invalid • Order immediate divorce • Enforce the implied relationship • Require the men to stand by their prior words

Lavender added softly,

"They owe us loyalty."

Leona wrote what they all agreed on:

"They will forget those women."

"They will love us."

Silence fell.

Even the room felt heavy.

Reality Ignored

One teacher hesitated.

"Can a court make someone love us?"

Lydia snapped,

"They already made them marry."

"So yes."

Lucinda nodded.

"Law can control behavior."

"Feelings follow."

Submitting the Papers

They walked to the courthouse.

Handed the documents to the clerk.

"Supreme Court appeal," Lydia said.

The clerk blinked.

"You sure?"

"Yes."

He stamped it.

The sound echoed like thunder.

Town Reaction

Word spread fast.

"They filed?"

"Supreme Court?"

"They bold."

"That ain't gonna work."

Some sympathized.

Others shook their heads.

"You can't force love."

The Protectors Hear

Preston read the rumor.

"They serious."

Paxton sighed.

"They want to erase our wives."

Phoenix clenched his jaw.

"Not happening."

Parker said quietly,

"Our covenant stands."

The Wives

Still silent.

Magnolia cooked.

Millicent folded laundry.

Marisol tended the garden.

Moonland prayed.

Margaret baked bread.

Miyako sewed.

Marigold laughed softly.

Their peace unsettled everyone.

Seven women sealed envelopes.

Seven men held their ground.

Seven marriages stood firm.

And the town waited.

Because now...

This wasn't just local drama.

It was national.

The Journey to Topeka

When the court date was finally set, everyone was stunned.

The appeal would be heard in Topeka, Kansas.

Not locally.

Not quietly.

But in a courtroom that carried national weight.

A two-day train ride from their town.

The notice read:

All parties must appear.

That meant:

The Protectors • Their wives • The seven teachers • The sheriff

Not the lower judge.

This was bigger than him now.

What a Test

Preston read the notice out loud.

"This is real," he said quietly.

Paxton shook his head. "Never thought we'd be going to a high court."

Phoenix whispered, "This is a trial."

Parker nodded. "Not just legal."

"Spiritual," Pierce added.

Porter sighed. "What a test of covenant."

Pablo whispered, "God sees."

Nationwide Attention

Newspapers across the country picked it up.

"FORCED MARRIAGES APPEALED" "TEACHERS SEEK COURT-ORDERED DIVORCE" "CAN THE LAW COMMAND LOVE?"

The town barber talked about it.

The preacher preached about it.

Women whispered in sewing circles.

Men debated in saloons.

It was everywhere.

Different Trains

They did not travel together.

Not out of fear.

But wisdom.

The teachers boarded one train.

Cold.

Silent.

Focused.

The Protectors and their wives boarded another train a day earlier.

They wanted peace first.

Arriving Early

Magnolia stepped off the train and breathed deep.

"Fresh air."

Millicent smiled. "Big city."

Marisol laughed. "We need shoes for this."

They checked into a hotel.

Clean.

Bright.

Safe.

That evening they walked.

Hand in hand.

Window shopping.

Street music.

Warm dinners.

Laughter.

For once...

No drama.

Quiet Moments

Paxton pulled Marigold aside.

"Thank you for standing with me."

She smiled softly. "I chose you."

Phoenix and Moonland sat on a bench.

"I'm proud of you," he said.

"For what?"

"For being strong."

She smiled.

Parker bought Millicent a small ribbon.

"Courtship never ends," he said shyly.

She laughed.

They prayed together in their rooms.

"Lord," Magnolia whispered, "You remember covenants."

"Cover us."

"Let truth stand."

The Teachers Arrive

The next day...

Another train pulled in.

The teachers stepped down.

Faces firm.

No smiles.

No laughter.

Only resolve.

Lydia whispered, "This is it."

Lucinda nodded. "We go all the way."

Loretta clenched her bag. "They'll have to hear us."

The Sheriff

The sheriff arrived on the same train travelling first class to avoid any disturbances.

Hat tipped low.

"This town sure know how to travel," he muttered.

He checked in.

Shook his head.

"Lord help us tomorrow."

Night Before Court

Both sides prayed.

In separate rooms.

Separate hearts.

One group praying for truth to stand.

The other praying for justice in their favor.

409

Topeka slept.

Unaware.

But morning would bring history.

This wasn't just about seven men.

Or seven women.

This was about:

authority • covenant • freedom • choice

And God was watching.

Chapter Fifthteen

The Supreme Court chamber felt cold.

Not from temperature.

From power.

Marble floors echoed each step. Wooden benches groaned under weight. Every whisper bounced off stone walls like judgment.

No one wore hats.

No one smiled.

This was not a place for comfort.

This was a place where lives were decided.

The Protectors

The seven men sat rigid.

Preston Protect Paxton Protect Phoenix Protect Parker Protect Pierce Protect Porter Protect Pablo Protect

Hands clasped.

Shoulders tight.

Jaws clenched.

Their wives sat across from them.

Quiet. Peaceful. Composed.

Faces calm.

Eyes steady.

They did not speak.

They did not react.

They simply sat.

The Teachers

Across the aisle...

Seven women sat together.

Lydia Teacher Lillian Teacher Lucinda
Teacher Louisa Teacher Loretta Teacher
Leona Teacher Lavender Teacher

Eyes swollen.

Hands shaking.

Tissues crushed.

They looked wounded.

But determined.

The Audience

Local attorneys packed the back rows.

Whispering urgently.

"This could overturn precedent." "If they rule for divorce..." "Hundreds of marriages affected." "This is dangerous territory."

No one laughed.

Court Begins

Black-robed judges entered.

Faces unreadable.

The gavel struck.

"Court is in session."

Silence fell.

Not respectful silence.

Fearful silence.

Teachers Speak

Lydia rose slowly.

Her voice trembled.

"Your Honors…"

"We were misled."

Tears slid down.

"We left our jobs."

"Our school."

"Our calling."

Lucinda stood.

"They invited us."

"They implied future."

"They gave us hope."

Loretta slammed her palm.

"We waited."

"We saved ourselves."

"We brought wedding dresses."

Leona sobbed.

"We thought God was working."

Lavender whispered.

"We trusted."

414

"They replaced us."

Pain Spills Out

Lydia cried,

"Do you know what it feels like..."

"To travel days believing you are loved?"

"To walk into a house..."

"And see your men hugging other women?"

Lillian screamed,

"We were HUMILIATED!"

Lucinda shouted,

"They dragged us outside!"

"They embarrassed us!"

Loretta sobbed,

"We were handled like animals!"

The courtroom stirred.

Gasps.

Murmurs.

Lawyers Whispers

"This is persuasive." "Public sympathy." "They might sway the bench."

Men Respond

Preston stood.

Hands trembling.

"Your Honors..."

"We never intended harm."

Paxton swallowed.

"We never promised marriage."

Phoenix spoke quietly.

"We never said we loved them."

Parker's voice cracked.

"We never knew they quit their jobs."

Pierce whispered.

"We never meant to hurt them."

Porter added.

"We were trying to defend ourselves."

Pablo wiped his face.

"We are sorry for their pain."

Teachers Push Back

Lydia snapped,

"Words don't erase betrayal!"

Lucinda cried,

"You planted dreams!"

Loretta shouted,

"You watched us fall in love!"

Leona sobbed,

"You let us wait!"

Lavender whispered,

"You let us believe!"

The Wives

Still silent.

Not one word.

Not one tear.

Magnolia's face soft.

Millicent peaceful.

Marisol composed.

Moonland prayerful.

Margaret steady.

Miyako gentle.

Marigold confident.

Their silence unsettled the room.

Tension Builds

One attorney whispered,

"This court could change history today."

Another muttered,

"This is dangerous."

Men Speak Again

Phoenix said quietly,

"We are not monsters."

Paxton added,

"We are not liars."

Parker whispered,

"We are human."

Pierce said,

"We made mistakes."

Porter nodded.

"We own them."

Pablo cried.

"But we won't accept false accusations."

Teachers Cry Harder

Lydia screamed,

"You owe us!"

Lucinda shouted,

"You ruined our future!"

Loretta cried,

"You should pay!"

Leona sobbed,

"We waited for you!"

Lavender whispered,

"We loved you!"

The Court Watches

Judges wrote.

Faces still stone.

No reaction.

No sympathy shown.

The room felt like it stopped breathing.

Closing Beat

This was bigger than love.

Bigger than heartbreak.

This was about power.

About authority.

About freedom.

And everyone waited...

For what the court would say next.

Behind Closed Doors

The chief judge leaned forward.

"Court will recess."

The gavel struck once.

"Judges will deliberate."

A collective gasp moved through the courtroom.

People shifted in their seats.

Hands clenched.

Tears paused mid-fall.

The three judges stood.

They were now locked in:

Judge Harold Whitcombe – senior justice, gray hair, stern eyes Judge Eleanor Fairchild – sharp-minded, composed, unreadable Judge Thomas Calder – younger, intense, analytical

They walked through a side door.

Heavy wood closed behind them.

Locked in.

Inside the Chambers

Judge Whitcombe removed his glasses.

"This is dangerous territory."

Judge Fairchild folded her hands.

"This case touches every forced marriage ruling."

Judge Calder paced.

"If we overturn…"

"Every ruling like this can be challenged."

Silence.

The weight pressed down.

Outside – The Waiting

Back in the courtroom…

No one spoke.

Teachers whispered prayers.

Lydia clenched her Bible.

Lucinda cried quietly.

Loretta stared at the door.

Leona rocked back and forth.

Lavender wiped her face.

The Men

Preston stared straight ahead.

Paxton flexed his jaw.

Phoenix clasped his hands tighter.

Parker swallowed hard.

Pierce exhaled slowly.

Porter leaned forward.

Pablo closed his eyes.

No hats.

No bravado.

Just nerves.

The Wives

Still silent.

Still composed.

Magnolia's face calm.

Millicent steady.

Marisol upright.

Moonland's lips moving in prayer.

Margaret peaceful.

Miyako serene.

Marigold confident.

They did not whisper.

They did not cry.

Their stillness unsettled everyone.

The Audience

Lawyers whispered.

"This could shake precedent."

"Whitcombe is conservative."

"Fairchild leans justice."

"Calder follows law strictly."

People leaned closer.

No one blinked.

Inside – Judges Deliberate

Whitcombe spoke.

"These women believed promises."

Fairchild answered.

"But belief is not contract."

Calder added.

"Implied relationship is not legal obligation."

Whitcombe sighed.

"The punishment..."

Fairchild interrupted.

"Was unusual."

Calder nodded.

"But legal under local statute."

Silence.

Long silence.

Tension Builds

Outside, Lydia whispered,

"They better see our pain."

Lucinda cried,

"They owe us justice."
425

Loretta hissed,

"They ruined us."

Leona whispered,

"God help us."

Lavender sobbed quietly.

The Door Remains Closed

Minutes felt like hours.

Footsteps echoed.

Someone coughed.

A reporter's pen dropped.

Every sound felt too loud.

Behind the door...

Three judges held lives in their hands.

Outside...

Fourteen hearts waited.

History waited.

The Condition

Behind closed doors, the three judges sat in silence.

Judge Whitcombe finally spoke.

"We have reached a decision."

Judge Fairchild nodded slowly. "Carefully considered."

Judge Calder exhaled. "With consequence."

They stood together.

Straightened their robes.

Opened the chamber door.

Back in the Courtroom

The heavy door creaked open.

Every head turned.

The room went still.

Not a whisper.

Not a breath.

Judge Whitcombe took his seat.

The gavel struck.

"Court is back in session."

Lydia gripped Lucinda's hand.

Loretta's lips trembled.

Leona whispered, "God..."

Lavender wiped her face.

Across the aisle, the men sat rigid.

The wives stayed silent.

Steady.

Unmoving.

The Judges Speak

Judge Whitcombe's voice cut through the room.

"We have reached a ruling."

The teachers leaned forward.

Reporters froze mid-scratch.

"We will grant the divorce order."

The teachers screamed.

Joy exploded.

"We knew it!" "Thank You, God!" "Yes!"

The men shook their heads slowly.

The wives did not move.

But Then...

Judge Whitcombe raised his hand.

"Order."

The room quieted.

"Only under one condition."

The air turned heavy.

Every eye locked on him.

Judge Fairchild leaned forward.

"We will grant the teachers' request in full."

Lucinda sobbed.

Loretta smiled wildly.

Leona whispered, "We won!"

Judge Calder continued:

"But only if..."

The pause was cruel.

"Each man signs the divorce decree right now."

Gasps.

"And immediately marries the teachers."

The room exploded again.

"Yes!" "They have to!" "They're ours!"

Judge Whitcombe finished:

"If the teachers are correct..."

"That you once had feelings."

"And that they can make you love them..."

"Then this court will reverse the marriages."

"You will sign willingly."

"You will leave your wives."

Silence fell.

Thick.

Heavy.

The men stood.

All seven.

At the same time.

The Stand

They turned.

Looked at their wives.

Not fear.

Not doubt.

Certainty.

In perfect unison they said loudly:

"WE WILL NOT LEAVE OUR WIVES." "WE LOVE THEM ONLY."

The courtroom ERUPTED.

Shouting. Gasping. Screaming.

The teachers fainted.

One collapsed.

Another screamed hysterically.

"You LIARS!" "You PROMISED!" "You CHEATED!"

They called the men names.

"Cowards!" "Traitors!" "Ungrateful!"

The sheriff rushed forward.

Clergy stood up.

"Lord have mercy!"

Reporters scribbled like mad.

This was history.

Order!

Judge Whitcombe slammed the gavel.

"ORDER!"

The noise barely lowered.

He struck again.

"ORDER IN THIS COURT!"

Silence crept back.

Barely.

Judge Fairchild stood.

"This court will not force hearts."

Judge Calder added:

"This case is dismissed."

Gavel slammed.

"DISMISSED."

Chaos

The room exploded again.

Cheers. Crying. Anger. Shock.

Church members clapped.

Teachers wailed.

Reporters ran out shouting headlines.

Town people whispered.

"This is history!" "They stood!" "Love won!"

The Couples

The men turned to their wives.

Held them.

Tight.

Tears fell.

Magnolia finally smiled.

Millicent wept quietly.

Marisol hugged hard.

Moonland whispered prayers.

Margaret laughed through tears.

Miyako held Pierce's face.

Marigold kissed Paxton's cheek.

Not shame.

Not fear.

Victory.

The teachers collapsed in grief.

The men stood firm.

The wives stood strong.

The judges watched silently.

History had been written.

Not by law.

By covenant.

After the Gavel Fell

The gavel had barely stopped echoing when the room exploded.

Cheers. Cries. Gasps. Reporters shouting questions.

But the loudest sounds...

Came from the teachers.

Lydia screamed, "THIS ISN'T OVER!"

Lucinda sobbed so hard she nearly collapsed. "They STOLE our lives!"

Loretta shouted, "God sees this injustice!"

Leona wailed, "We waited for them!"

Lavender cried, "We gave everything!"

Their voices clashed against the roar of the crowd.

The Couples

The Protectors turned instantly.

No hesitation.

They pulled their wives into their arms.

Tight. Protective. Unashamed.

Preston held Magnolia like he never wanted to let go. Paxton kissed Marigold's forehead. Phoenix pressed Moonland close. Parker hugged Millicent until she laughed through tears. Pierce held Miyako's face gently. Porter wrapped Margaret in his coat. Pablo lifted Marisol slightly off the floor, spinning once in joy.

The crowd gasped.

The kisses were not scandalous.

They were victorious.

Covenant.

Public.

Unashamed.

Teachers Break

The teachers lost it.

Lydia screamed, "LOOK AT THEM!"

Lucinda shrieked, "THEY'RE MOCKING US!"

Loretta lunged forward.

"GET OFF HER!"

Leona followed.

Lavender rushed behind them.

"They're OURS!"

Chaos Erupts

They surged forward.

Not graceful.

Not controlled.

Pure emotion.

Hands reaching.

Voices screaming.

"LET US THROUGH!" "YOU OWE US!"
"THIS ISN'T FAIR!"

Court officers jumped in.

"STOP!" "BACK UP!"

The teachers fought against them.

Crying.

Kicking.

Trying to push past.

The Protectors immediately stepped in front of their wives.

Preston shouted, "Don't touch them!"

Paxton raised his hands.

"Back away!"

Phoenix barked, "Enough!"

Arrests

The officers had no choice.

"Lydia Teacher, you are under arrest." "Lucinda Teacher, under arrest." "Loretta, Leona, Lavender—step back NOW!"

Handcuffs snapped.

The teachers screamed.

"You can't do this!" "This is persecution!" "God will judge you!"

One collapsed to the floor crying.

Another spit words of rage.

The Judge Steps In

Judge Whitcombe rose.

"Order!"

His voice boomed.

"Remove them."

"They will spend the night in custody."

Gasps.

The teachers screamed louder.

"No!" "You can't lock us up!" "We're victims!"

Judge Fairchild added calmly,

"This court will not tolerate violence."

Judge Calder said,

"Escort them."

Restraining Order

The sheriff stepped forward.

"Your Honors," he said respectfully, "Given the hostility..."

"I request a restraining order."

Judge Whitcombe nodded.

"So ordered."

He read slowly:

"These women are hereby prohibited from coming within 1,500 feet of the Protectors and their wives."

Gasps filled the room.

Teachers screamed.

"You're protecting THEM again!" "This is bias!" "You hate us!"

The gavel slammed.

"Enough."

Dragged Away

The teachers were pulled toward the exit.

Crying. Screaming. Begging.

"This is injustice!" "You'll pay for this!" "We'll appeal again!"

Their voices echoed down the hallway.

Then silence.

The Room After

The courtroom felt emptier.

But heavier.

The wives clung to their husbands.

Magnolia whispered, "It's over."

Millicent breathed out. "We're safe."

Marisol said softly, "God did this."

Moonland prayed quietly. "Thank You, Jesus."

Margaret wiped tears. "He kept covenant."

Miyako smiled. "We made it."

Marigold laughed softly. "Did y'all see their faces?"

Reporters

Flash questions flew.

"How do you feel?" "Do you fear retaliation?" "Was this love?"

Preston answered calmly,

"We stand on covenant."

Paxton added,

"God defended us."

Phoenix said,

"We're grateful."

As they walked out...

Hands held tight.

Heads high.

Love public.

Victory loud.

Behind them...

The jail doors closed.

And seven broken women cried in the dark.

But in the light...

Seven marriages stood unshaken.

Chapter Sixteen

Unexpected Open Doors

The night the teachers spent in custody was not what anyone expected.

Instead of silence...

Instead of shame...

The telegrams began arriving.

One after another.

The sheriff's office clerk rushed in, arms full.

"Sheriff... you better see this."

He laid them across the desk.

Dozens.

Then more.

And more.

Soon the table was covered.

The Messages

Lydia read the first one out loud:

NEED STRONG TEACHERS. POSITION
OPEN IMMEDIATELY. FIRST CLASS
TRAVEL PROVIDED.

Lucinda gasped.

Another read:

WE WILL HOUSE YOU. GOOD SALARY.
SAFE COMMUNITY.

Loretta laughed.

"They want us!"

Leona opened another:

MANY GOD-FEARING MEN HERE
SEEKING WIVES.

Lavender blushed.

"They know we're pure."

Another said:

TRAIN FARE PAID. FIRST CLASS. COME
SOON.

The room filled with excitement.

Their Reputation Changed

They had arrived in Topeka heartbroken.

But now...

They were wanted.

Every town needed teachers.

Every community was desperate for women of character.

Their public stand had gone nationwide.

Newspapers called them:

"Faithful Women" "Women of Conviction" "Courageous Teachers"

They were celebrities.

A New Focus

The teachers forgot the Protectors.

Forgot the court.

Forgot the anger.

They laughed.

Cried happy tears.

"This is God," Lydia whispered.

Lucinda nodded.

"He didn't forget us."

Loretta laughed.

"We thought we lost everything."

Leona said softly,

"And He gave us more."

Their Luggage

Their trunks were already packed.

They had moved out of the boardinghouse.

They were ready.

"Where should we go?" Lavender asked.

They sat around the table that night, telegrams spread out.

Arguing playfully.

"This one pays more." "This town looks prettier." "They have a big church." "They promised a house!"

They spent the entire evening choosing.

Dinner sat untouched.

They were too excited to eat.

A Decision

"We shouldn't rush," Lydia said.

"We're staying here tonight."

"In Topeka," Lucinda added.

"We'll pray."

"We'll decide."

They agreed.

They would stay at the boardinghouse in Topeka.

Sleep on it.

Let God lead.

Kindness Everywhere

People recognized them.

Shopkeepers gave them discounts.

Women hugged them.

Men tipped their hats respectfully.

"You did right," someone whispered.

"You stood for yourself."

They were treated like honor guests.

Scripture Remembered

That night, Lavender opened her Bible.

Read aloud:

"O the depth of the riches both of the wisdom and knowledge of God! How unsearchable are His judgments, and His ways past finding out!" — Romans 11:33

They all went quiet.

"That's it," Leona whispered.

"God's ways."

Hope Renewed

Lydia smiled through tears.

"We thought we were rejected."

Lucinda said softly,

"But He redirected us."

Loretta laughed.

"We almost begged men who didn't want us."

Leona smiled.

"And now whole towns want us."

Lavender whispered,

"Jesus didn't forget."

Closing Beat

That night...

Seven women sat around a table.

Not broken.

Not bitter.

But hopeful.

Telegrams stacked high.

Suitcases packed.

Dreams restored.

They were embarking on a new life.

Not chasing love.

But walking into purpose.

And God...

Was writing their next chapter.

Chapter Seventeen

Chosen, Booked, and Bound for a New Town**

For several days straight, the teachers did nothing but write and receive telegrams.

Morning.

Noon.

Night.

The clerk at the telegraph office finally laughed.

"You ladies again?"

Lydia smiled proudly. "We're in demand."

Lucinda opened another message:

GENEROUS SALARY. PRIVATE HOUSE PROVIDED. LARGE SCHOOL DISTRICT.

Loretta squealed. "That's the one!"

Leona read another:

SEVERAL WEALTHY CATTLE BARONS SEEKING GOD-FEARING WIVES.

Lavender fanned herself. "They want us."

Still a Little Delusional

They gathered around the table.

"We're pure women," Lydia said confidently.

Lucinda nodded. "Set apart."

Loretta added, "Men want that."

But Leona hesitated.

"Nobody's pure but Jesus," she said softly.

"All have sinned."

Lavender waved her off.

"We're celebrities now."

"They see us as special."

They laughed.

Their confidence had grown almost too much.

Choosing the Town

They finally selected one telegram.

Town locked in: Cedar Ridge, Colorado

A wealthy ranch town.

Large schoolhouse.

Strong church.

And rumors of powerful cattle barons.

"They pay double," Loretta said.

"And a house," Lucinda added.

"And first-class travel," Lavender squealed.

They sent their acceptance.

Waiting for Travel

First-class seats were limited.

They were placed on a waiting list.

Five days.

"That's fine," Lydia said.

"We deserve rest."

They shopped.

Ate well.

Were recognized everywhere.

People asked for autographs.

They loved it.

Farewell Press Release

On the day of departure...

They called reporters.

"We want a farewell," Lydia said.

Cameras flashed.

Town people gathered.

Lucinda wiped her eyes dramatically.

"This is a new beginning."

Loretta smiled.

"We're grateful."

Leona added,

"God did this."

Lavender declared,

"We're walking into destiny."

Boarding the Train

Their trunks were heavy.

New dresses.

New dreams.

They stepped onto the train.

First class.

Velvet seats.

Curtains.

Champagne offered.

They laughed.

"This is the life," Loretta said.

A New Beginning

As the train pulled away...

They waved.

Crowds cheered.

Reporters snapped photos.

Topeka faded behind them.

Truth Underneath

But the narrator whispered quietly...

They were still broken.

Still learning.

Still human.

Still imperfect.

As Scripture says:

"For all have sinned, and come short of the glory of God." — Romans 3:23

They forgot that part.

For now.

Seven women rode west.

Famous.

Confident.

Excited.

Thinking they had won.

But God...

Was still writing their story.

And Cedar Ridge, Colorado had no idea who was coming.

What They Never Asked

The telegram from Cedar Ridge, Colorado sounded perfect.

Beautiful home. Excellent salary. Three-year contract. Wealthy cattle barons backing the school.

The teachers never asked one question.

Who are we teaching?

They saw:

Money • Prestige • Comfort • Status

And they signed.

Three years.

Ink dried.

Contract sealed.

Their Arrival

When they arrived in Cedar Ridge, a carriage waited.

Polished.

Driver in a pressed coat.

They smiled.

"We made it."

They were taken to a large house.

Wrap-around porch. Fresh curtains. Fully furnished. Coal stove burning warm.

"This is ours," Lydia whispered.

Lucinda touched the drapes. "Luxury."

Loretta laughed. "We deserve this."

The Surprise Meeting

That evening, the cattle barons arrived.

Tall men.

Well dressed.

Boots polished.

They shook hands.

"Welcome."

"You'll start tomorrow."

Leona asked casually, "How many students?"

One man paused.

"About thirty."

"Children?" Lavender asked.

The men exchanged glances.

"No."

Silence fell.

Lydia frowned. "Then... who?"

The cattleman cleared his throat.

"Women."

Who They Were Teaching

He continued slowly.

"Widows."

Lucinda blinked.

"Former dancers."

Loretta stiffened.

"Abused wives."

Leona swallowed.

"Reformed soiled doves."

Lavender gasped.

459

"Single mothers."

The room went still.

"These women survived life," he finished.

"They can't read."

"They can't write."

"They want dignity."

"They want scripture."

"They want a future."

Shock

The teachers stared.

"But... we thought..." Loretta began.

"School," Lydia whispered.

"Children," Lucinda said.

The cattleman shook his head.

"No."

"These women need teachers."

"Like you."

Reality Hits

They looked at each other.

This wasn't what they imagined.

No classrooms of obedient children.

No pretty desks.

No spelling bees.

These were women:

Broken. Scarred. Strong. Survivors.

Leona whispered,

"They lived the life we judged."

Lavender felt her chest tighten.

"God..."

The Contract

The cattleman placed papers on the table.

"You signed."

"Three years."

"Good salary."

"Safe home."

"You agreed."

Lydia stared at the ink.

Her own signature.

Lucinda whispered,

"We never asked."

Loretta said softly,

"We were blinded by money."

Divine Irony

They had stood in court calling themselves pure.

Now...

Former dancers.

Soiled doves.

Women who had been used.

Discarded.

Forgotten.

God's Hand

Leona whispered,

"God did this."

Lucinda nodded.

"He's humbling us."

Loretta wiped her eyes.

"He's showing us ourselves."

Lavender whispered,

"We're not better."

Their First Class

The next morning...

Thirty women walked in.

Different ages.

Different races.

In another season.

In another story.

Lydia finally whispered:

"God resisteth the proud, but giveth grace unto the humble." — James 4:6

They bowed their heads.

This...

Was their true assignment.

Not money.

Not fame.

Redemption.

Chapter Seventeen

The House on Hawthorne Hill

That night, the teachers sat in silence in the parlor of the beautiful home provided for them.

Soft lamplight glowed against cream-colored walls. Heavy drapes hung perfectly pressed. A thick rug warmed their bare feet.

They were staying on land owned by the wealthiest cattle baron in Cedar Ridge.

Silas Hawthorne – owner of Hawthorne Ranch Wife: Esther Hawthorne – former soiled dove, now a community leader

Silas Hawthorne was an older gentleman. Silver hair. Deep voice. Eyes full of wisdom.

Esther Hawthorne...

She carried quiet strength.

She had once lived the life.

But she found grace in Silas' eyes.

He did not judge her. He did not shame her. He saw her worth.

He married her.

And she changed the town.

Esther's Legacy

Esther opened:

A school for women • A sewing house • A bakery cooperative • A small market stall district

She helped women:

Work. Earn. Save. Open businesses.

The women of Cedar Ridge called her:

"Mother Esther."

Silas practically owned the town.

Not by fear.

By generosity.

That Night

After dinner, the Hawthornes retired to their wing of the house.

The teachers sat alone.

No laughter.

Just silence.

Lydia finally spoke.

"This... isn't what I expected."

Lucinda hugged a pillow.

"We thought children."

Loretta stared at the fire.

"We thought chalkboards and spelling."

Leona whispered,

"We thought prestige."

Lavender swallowed.

"We didn't ask one question."

Their Fear

Lucinda said quietly,

"I don't know how to teach these women."

Loretta nodded.

"I've never been around..."

She hesitated.

"These types."

Leona whispered,

"We lived sheltered lives."

Lavender added softly,

"Pure."

"Untouched."

They sat with that word.

Pure.

They had said it so proudly before.

Now it felt...

Small.

Reality Hits

"These women lived," Lydia whispered.

"They survived."

"They were hurt."

Lucinda said,

"We don't know their world."

Loretta rubbed her arms.

"What if they hate us?"

Leona added,

"What if they smell judgment?"

Lavender whispered,

"We don't belong."

Conviction

A silence fell.

Then Leona spoke again.

"Esther belonged."

They all looked up.

"She lived that life."

"And God redeemed her."

"She teaches them."

"She leads them."

Lydia whispered,

"God placed us here."

Lucinda nodded slowly.

"To humble us."

Loretta sighed.

"To stretch us."

Lavender wiped her eyes.

"To break pride."

Scripture

Lydia opened her Bible.

Read softly:

"And whosoever shall exalt himself shall be abased; and he that shall humble himself shall be exalted." — Matthew 23:12

They sat quietly.

Honesty

Loretta finally said it.

"We thought we were better."

Lucinda nodded.

"We judged."

Leona whispered,

"We called ourselves pure."

Lavender added,

"But only Jesus is."

They bowed their heads.

Prayer

Lydia prayed:

"Lord... we don't know what we're doing."

"But You do."

"Help us see them like You see them."

"Not past."

"But purpose."

"Not shame."

"But destiny."

"Amen."

They climbed the stairs slowly.

Each to her room.

Soft beds.

Clean sheets.

Luxury.

But their hearts...

Were heavy.

Tomorrow...

They would face women .

And for the first time...

They realized...

They were the ones who needed teaching.

The Night Before Everything Changed

The teachers sat long after the lamps had dimmed.

Outside, crickets sang.

Wind brushed the tall grass around Hawthorne Ranch.

Inside...

Seven women wrestled with reality.

Lydia finally broke the silence again.

"We really thought God brought us here for children."

Lucinda shook her head slowly.

"We pictured little desks."

"Little shoes by the door."

"Spelling bees."

Loretta sighed.

"And clean hands."

Leona whispered,

"But instead..."

"Scarred hands."

Lavender added,

"Hands that have held too much."

Fear Surfaces

Lucinda hugged herself.

"I don't know how to talk to them."

"What if they curse?"

"What if they're angry?"

Loretta whispered,

"What if they hate us?"

"What if they see right through us?"

473

Leona said quietly,

"They will."

Lavender nodded.

"They lived."

"They survived."

"They're strong."

The Weight of Pride

Lydia leaned back.

"We were proud."

Lucinda nodded.

"We thought we were chosen."

Loretta added,

"We liked the fame."

Leona whispered,

"We liked being admired."

Lavender said softly,

"We forgot humility."

Esther's Story Returns

Loretta glanced toward the closed hallway.

"Esther didn't forget."

Lucinda whispered,

"She lived it."

Leona added,

"She understands."

Lavender said,

"She looks at those women…"

"Like daughters."

Conviction Deepens

Lydia opened her Bible again.

Her voice shook.

"Judge not, that ye be not judged." — Matthew 7:1

Silence.

Lucinda whispered,

"We judged."

Loretta nodded.

"We called ourselves different."

Leona added,

"We made ourselves better."

Lavender swallowed.

"But God…"

"He put us right here."

Unspoken Fear

Loretta finally admitted,

"What if they reject us?"

Lucinda said,

"They might."

Leona added,

"They have every right."

Lavender whispered,

"We sound like Pharisees."

Breaking Point

Lydia covered her face.

"I don't want to fail."

Lucinda cried quietly.

"What if they laugh at us?"

Loretta said,

"What if they leave?"

Leona added,

"What if they don't trust us?"

Lavender whispered,

"What if they see through the nice dresses?"

Prayer Again

They knelt.

Carpet under knees.

Hands joined.

"Lord..."

"Strip our pride."

"Take away fear."

"Help us love."

"Not teach."

"But serve."

"Let us wash feet."

"Not stand tall."

"Make us small."

"Amen."

Down the Hall

Unseen...

Esther Hawthorne stood by the stairwell.

She had heard everything.

Her eyes filled.

She whispered to herself,

"Thank You, Jesus."

Esther Speaks

She entered quietly.

"You're scared."

They jumped.

"Mrs. Hawthorne..."

Esther smiled gently.

"I was too."

"When I started."

Lucinda whispered,

"You understand."

Esther nodded.

"I lived it."

Loretta swallowed.

"We don't know what to do."

Esther sat.

"Then listen."

Esther's Wisdom

"Don't teach first."

"Listen."

"Let them talk."

"Let them cry."

"Let them be angry."

"Don't correct."

"Don't fix."

"Just stay."

Lydia whispered,

"We thought we had answers."

Esther smiled.

"You don't."

"Neither do they."

"Jesus does."

Truth Spoken

"You lived sheltered," Esther said gently.

"They lived storm."

"But both need grace."

Leona whispered,

"We thought we were better."

Esther shook her head.

"No one is."

Final Words of the Night

Esther stood.

"Tomorrow..."

"You meet queens."

"Not broken women."

"Queens who survived."

"Honor them."

Then she left.

The teachers sat still.

Hearts pounding.

Tomorrow...

Everything would change.

Not for the students.

But for them.

Chapter Eighteen

Women Who Came to Learn

Morning came softly over Cedar Ridge.

Sunlight spilled through the windows of the small schoolroom on Hawthorne land. The air smelled of clean wood and fresh chalk.

The teachers stood quietly near the board.

Simple dresses. Hair pinned neatly. Hands folded.

They were nervous.

But ready.

The Students Arrive

The door opened.

Women entered one by one.

Different ages. Different races. Some with scars on their hands. Some with tired eyes.

But all had the same look.

Determination.

They did not laugh. They did not talk loudly. They sat down quietly at the long tables.

Books opened. Pencils ready.

They came for one reason.

To learn.

No Stories Today

No one spoke of the past.

No one cried.

No one asked for sympathy.

They didn't want pity.

They wanted progress.

They had work to do after class.

Money to make.

Lives to rebuild.

They only had four hours.

Three days a week.

And they would not waste a minute.

Teachers Observe

Lydia watched them carefully.

"They're serious," she whispered.

Lucinda nodded.

"They came prepared."

Loretta said softly,

"They're hungry... for knowledge."

Leona whispered,

"Not attention."

Lavender added,

"They want tools."

Class Begins

Esther Hawthorne walked in.

"Good morning, ladies."

The women stood respectfully.

"Good morning, Mrs. Hawthorne."

She smiled.

"Sit."

They obeyed.

She turned to the teachers.

"Begin."

The First Lesson

Lydia walked to the board.

Wrote slowly:

A

She turned.

"This is A."

The women repeated together.

"A."

No laughter.

No joking.

Just focus.

She wrote:

B C D

They followed.

Writing.

Sounding.

Learning.

Quiet Hunger

One woman leaned closer to her book.

Another practiced her letters again and again.

A third whispered the sounds to herself.

No one complained.

No one distracted.

This was their chance.

Why They Were Here

They didn't stay after class.

They didn't linger.

When the lesson ended...

They stood.

Thanked the teachers.

And rushed out.

Work awaited.

Cleaning houses. Cooking. Sewing. Selling goods.

Education was a tool.

Not entertainment.

Teachers Changed

After they left...

The room felt holy.

Lucinda whispered,

"They don't waste time."

Loretta nodded.

"They're building."

Leona said quietly,

"We were wrong."

Lavender added,

"They're stronger than we thought."

Esther's Wisdom

Esther said softly,

"They came to learn."

"Not be saved."

"Not be judged."

"Just equipped."

Scripture

Lydia opened her Bible.

"Wisdom is the principal thing; therefore get wisdom." — Proverbs 4:7

They nodded.

The teachers sat quietly.

Changed.

Humbled.

These women were not broken.

They were building.

And for the first time...

The teachers understood.

This was real ministry.

The following week while in the classroom.

Lydia stood in the doorway, arms folded.

"Well," she said quietly, "looks like class is canceled today."

Loretta leaned against the frame. "Storm said take a break."

The storm kind of made a mess of things after the women surveyed the destruction on the next day.

Lucinda smiled softly. "God still sent us here."

Leona scanned the sky. "It's clearing."

Lavender sighed. "But the roof isn't."

Louisa whispered, "It will need fixing"

Lillian nodded. "Somehow."

The Men Arrive

Hoofbeats.

Boots.

Voices.

Seven men came down the dirt road together.

Different walks. Different builds. Same purpose.

Elias Carter – uniform crisp, badge shining • Thomas Reed – tool belt low on his hips • Caleb Monroe – hauling long planks • Noah Blackbear – surveying the land • Henry Whitlock – awkward but eager • Samuel Park – notebook tucked under his arm • Jonathan Hale – quiet, observing

Lydia whispered, "Looks like help came."

Loretta smirked, "From heaven or trouble?"

Lucinda laughed softly, "Both."

First Words

Elias removed his hat.

"Ladies. Heard about the storm damage."

Lydia nodded. "Appreciate you coming, Sheriff."

He noticed her calm authority. The way she didn't need to raise her voice.

Something about her steadied him.

Thomas shifted nervously.

"I, uh... I can rebuild the desks."

Lucinda smiled. "Thank you."

He turned red instantly.

She noticed.

Caleb dropped lumber near Loretta.

"You always work this hard?"

She smirked. "Only when men are watching."

He froze.

She laughed.

Something stirred in him.

Noah nodded toward Leona.

"Storm didn't scare you."

She met his eyes. "I've seen worse."

He nodded once.

Respect.

Henry adjusted his coat.

"I can cover material costs if you want."

Lavender studied him. "You don't look like a supervisor."

He swallowed. "I came to help."

She smiled slightly.

Samuel looked at Lillian.

"You teach here?"

"Yes."

He scribbled.

"Mind if I write about it?"

She raised an eyebrow. "Depends what you write."

Challenge accepted.

Jonathan watched Louisa.

Her posture. Her presence.

She noticed him watching.

"You're quiet."

"I listen."

She smiled. "That's rare."

Working Together

No flirting.

Just purpose.

The men climbed ladders. Lifted beams. Replaced shingles.

The women directed.

"Thomas, that board goes there." "Caleb, hold it steady." "Noah, check that side." "Henry, nails are here."

Samuel wrote.

Jonathan watched.

Elias kept order.

Energy Shifts

Loretta handed Caleb water. "Thanks."

"You don't look like you need help."

She smiled. "Still nice to have it."

Lucinda corrected Thomas gently. "That joint needs tightening."

He nodded.

"You're smarter than me."

She laughed. "No. Just experienced."

Leona and Noah worked silently.

No wasted words.

Just rhythm.

Lavender watched Henry struggle. "You want help?"

He froze.

"Uh... yes."

She smiled.

He felt exposed.

But grateful.

Lillian leaned over Samuel's notes. "Write truth."

He met her gaze. "I intend to."

Louisa stood beside Jonathan. "You didn't have to come."

"I wanted to."

She smiled. "That's different."

By sunset...

The roof stood solid. Desks repaired. Windows sealed.

The school was strong again.

Lydia looked around. "Thank you."

Elias tipped his hat.

"Anytime."

No promises.

No flirting.

Just respect.

But something had shifted.

Energy. Possibility. God moving quietly.

Social Meetups Begin

1. Church Fellowship Dinner

The first gathering happened at church.

Long wooden tables. Home-cooked food. Soft hymns.

Elias sat near Lydia.

"You organize like a commander," he said.

She smiled. "Someone has to."

He nodded. "I admire that."

Thomas nervously passed bread to Lucinda.

"You built the new shelves," she said.

"Yeah... crooked maybe."

She laughed. "They hold books. That's what matters."

Caleb and Loretta stood near the coffee pot.

"You always joking," he said.

"That how I survive," she answered.

He nodded slowly. "I need some of that."

Noah and Leona sat outside on the steps.

"Your faith quiet," she said.

"Still water runs deep," he replied.

She smiled. "I see it."

Henry watched Lavender read announcements.

"You read strong," he said.

She noticed his pause.

"You want me to help you sometime?"

His face flushed.

"I would like that."

Samuel asked Lillian about the school.

"You write sharp," she said.

"You teach sharper," he answered.

Jonathan offered Louisa a seat.

"You changed that school," he said.

"It changed me," she replied.

2. Town Picnics

Blankets. Baskets. Music.

Elias walked Lydia to the creek.

"I buried my wife here," he admitted.

She squeezed his hand.

"You still believe in love?"

"I'm starting to again."

Thomas carved Lucinda a wooden bookmark.

"For your Bible."

She nearly cried.

Caleb admitted his accident.

A man was hurt on the rails."

Loretta said gently, "Jesus forgives."

He broke.

Noah showed Leona his tracking skills.

She laughed. "You quiet men see everything."

Henry confessed his secret.

"I can't read well."

Lavender took his hand.

"We'll fix that."

Samuel asked Lillian permission to write about her.

"Only if you write truth."

"I will."

Jonathan and Louisa spoke of land.

"I believe women should own property."

She smiled. "You're different."

3. Evening Walks

Small talks.

Shared laughter.

Quiet prayers.

Trust grew.

Then Proposals

Elias & Lydia

Under a cottonwood tree.

"I want to protect your heart," he said.

"Yes," she whispered.

Thomas & Lucinda

In the schoolhouse.

"Build a life with me?"

She nodded through tears.

Caleb & Loretta

At sunset.

"You forgive me?"

She kissed his cheek.

"Yes."

Noah & Leona

By the river.

"Our people honor covenant," he said.

She smiled. "So do I."

Henry & Lavender

In the bank office.

"Teach me forever."

She laughed. "Yes."

Samuel & Lillian

Outside the newspaper office.

"Write our story."

She nodded. "Yes."

Jonathan & Louisa

On the ranch hill.

"Stand with me."

She answered, "Always."

Weddings

Seven weddings.

Same month.

Different styles.

Church bells rang.

Children threw flowers.

The town celebrated.

Vows

They promised:

Protection • Faithfulness • Leadership • Honor
• Prayer

Final Scene

The women stood together.

Married.

Loved.

Chosen.

Not forced.

Chosen.

Lydia whispered,

"We waited for real men."

Lucinda smiled. "God delivered."

Loretta laughed. "Better than expected."

Leona added, "He heals everything."

Lavender said softly, "Even pride."

Lillian smiled. "Even fear."

Louisa concluded, "Even destiny."

Closing Scripture

"He who finds a wife finds a good thing, and obtains favor from the Lord." — Proverbs 18:22

Book Club Discussion Questions

Religion vs. Relationship**

Opening Reflection

What did this novel teach you about the difference between religion and relationship with God?

Which characters relied more on rules than on love? How did that affect their decisions?

At what point in the story did you personally recognize the shift from performance to genuine faith?

Purity & Judgment

How did the idea of "purity" become a weapon in this story?

Who defined purity in the novel—and who challenged that definition?

Do you think the teachers initially confused moral behavior with spiritual maturity? Why?

How does the Bible verse "all have sinned and fall short of the glory of God" change the way we view purity?

Why do you think society places higher value on sexual pasts than on present character?

In what ways did pride disguise itself as holiness in the story?

Religion vs. Relationship

Which moments showed characters obeying rules instead of following love?

How did Jesus' example contrast with the religious attitudes shown?

Why do you think people sometimes feel safer following rules than building relationships?

Have you ever experienced religious rejection? How did it affect your faith?

Grace & Redemption

Which character showed the greatest transformation?

How did grace—not condemnation—change lives in this novel?

Why is it harder to accept grace than judgment?

What role did forgiveness play in healing relationships?

Women & Identity

How were women misjudged because of their past?

What did the novel teach about worth beyond history?

How did God redefine these women's identities?

Marriage & Covenant

What does this novel teach about covenant vs. convenience?

How did the men grow in their understanding of love and leadership?

Why is choosing love daily more important than how a relationship starts?

Personal Application

Have you ever used religion to avoid vulnerability?

What area of your life needs relationship instead of rules?

Do you struggle more with judging others or judging yourself?

What does God's grace look like in your daily life?

Final Reflection

What line or moment stayed with you the most?

How did this story challenge your own beliefs?

If Jesus were physically present in one scene, which would it be—and why?

Closing Scripture Reflection

"For by grace are ye saved through faith; and that not of yourselves: it is the gift of God." — Ephesians 2:8

Discuss: • Why is grace difficult to accept? • How does this verse apply to the novel?

1890s recipes

1. Prairie Chicken & Dumplings

Ingredients: Whole chicken, flour, salt, pepper, onions, carrots, lard

Method: Simmer chicken with onions and carrots until tender. Roll flour dough thin, cut into strips, drop into broth. Cook until dumplings puff. Season well.

Served at community tables and boardinghouses.

2. Cast Iron Skillet Cornbread

Ingredients: Cornmeal, flour, eggs, buttermilk, lard, salt

Method: Heat greased skillet in oven. Mix batter. Pour into hot pan. Bake until golden.

Staple food on every ranch.

3. Salt Pork & Bean Stew

Ingredients: Dried beans, salt pork, onion, molasses

Method: Soak beans overnight. Simmer with pork and onions for hours. Sweeten lightly with molasses.

Filling winter meal.

4. Sourdough Biscuits

Ingredients: Sourdough starter, flour, lard, salt

Method: Mix dough, roll out. Cut rounds. Bake in hot oven.

Served with every meal.

5. Frontier Beef Pot Roast

Ingredients: Beef chuck, potatoes, carrots, onions, bay leaf

Method: Brown meat. Add vegetables. Cover and slow cook for hours.

Sunday dinner favorite.

6. Pioneer Apple Brown Betty

Ingredients: Dried apples, breadcrumbs, sugar, cinnamon

Method: Layer apples and crumbs. Bake until bubbling.

Simple dessert.

7. Milk Gravy Over Biscuits

Ingredients: Flour, bacon grease, milk, salt, pepper

Method: Make roux with grease and flour. Add milk. Serve over biscuits.

Common breakfast.

8. Stewed Dried Peaches

Ingredients: Dried peaches, sugar, cloves

Method: Simmer fruit until soft. Lightly sweeten.

Served warm.

9. Lard Pie Crust

Ingredients: Flour, lard, cold water, salt

Method: Cut lard into flour. Add water. Roll thin.

Used for all pies.

10. Frontier Beef Broth

Ingredients: Beef bones, onion, celery, salt, pepper

Method: Simmer bones 6-8 hours. Strain.

Healing food for sick and hungry.

Bonus Authentic Touches

Coffee boiled in enamel pots • Bread baked in Dutch ovens • Butter churned by hand • Eggs gathered daily • Milk fresh from cows

How To Start A Christian Book Club

1. Define Your Purpose

Ask first:

Is this for spiritual growth? • Fellowship? • Healing? • Women only? Mixed group? • Fiction, Bible studies, or both?

Example purpose statement: "Our book club exists to grow in Christ through reading, discussion, prayer, and community."

2. Choose Your Format

Decide:

In-person, online, or hybrid • Weekly, bi-weekly, or monthly • Home, church, café, or library • 60 or 90 minutes

3. Select Your First Book

Choose something:

Faith-centered • Easy to read • Discussion-worthy • Not too long

Good starters:

A Christian novel • A devotional • A grace-based book • Your own novel (perfect for outreach)

4. Invite Members

Ways to invite:

Church announcements • Facebook groups • Flyers • Word of mouth • Book signings • Women's ministry

Sample invite: "Join our Christian Book Club! We read, pray, and grow together."

5. Set Group Guidelines

Establish:

Respect • Confidentiality • No judgment • Everyone may speak • Grace over debate

6. Structure Each Meeting

Opening (10 minutes) • Welcome • Prayer • Icebreaker

Discussion (40 minutes) • Book questions • Scripture connections • Life application

Closing (10 minutes) • Prayer requests • Blessing

7. Sample Meeting Flow

Opening prayer

Check-in

Discussion questions

Scripture reflection

Prayer circle

8. Use Faith-Centered Questions

Ask:

Where did you see God in this chapter? • What challenged you? • How does this apply to your walk? • What scripture connects?

9. Grow the Club

Rotate facilitators • Invite guest speakers • Host author nights • Serve the community together • Start prayer chains

10. Keep It Grace-Based

Remember:

Not everyone is at the same faith level • No pressure to perform • Love first • Teach gently • Pray often

Scripture Foundation

"Where two or three are gathered in My name, there am I among them." — Matthew 18:20

Sample Club Covenant

"We commit to love, listen, pray, and grow together in Christ."

Bonus Ideas

Theme nights • Worship music • Testimony nights • Outreach projects • Book giveaways

How to Start A Farmers Market

1. Clarify Your Vision

Ask:

Why are we starting this market? • Food access? • Local business growth? • Community fellowship? • Faith-based outreach?

Example vision: "To provide fresh food, support local growers, and build community."

2. Choose a Location

Ideal places:

Church parking lots • Downtown squares • Community parks • Vacant lots • School grounds

Make sure:

Easy parking • Foot traffic • Shade or tents • Restrooms nearby

3. Secure Permissions

Check with:

City hall • Parks department • Property owners

You may need:

Event permit • Vendor license • Health department approval • Insurance

4. Pick a Schedule

Decide:

Weekly or bi-weekly • Saturday mornings are best • 3–4 hour window

Consistency builds trust.

5. Recruit Vendors

Invite:

Local farmers • Bakers • Honey producers • Jam makers • Soap crafters • Candle makers • Flower growers

Start small.

Quality > Quantity.

6. Set Market Rules

Create simple guidelines:

Local only • No reselling • Clean booths • Friendly conduct • No loud music • Setup & breakdown times

7. Pricing & Booth Fees

Options:

Free (community outreach) • $10–$25 per booth • Donation-based

Use fees for:

Signs • Trash pickup • Advertising

8. Marketing Your Market

Promote through:

Church announcements • Facebook groups • Flyers • Local radio • Schools • Word of mouth

Create a:

Market name • Simple logo • Consistent posting schedule

9. Market Day Setup

You'll need:

Tables • Tents • Weights • Signage • Trash cans • Handwashing station

Assign volunteers:

Setup crew • Welcome table • Vendor support

10. Add Community Touches

Make it special:

Live worship music • Prayer booth • Kids craft table • Cooking demos • Free samples

11. Safety & Cleanliness

Keep food covered • Trash removal • Hand sanitizer • First aid kit

12. Grow Slowly

After a few weeks:

Survey shoppers • Add vendors • Invite food trucks • Host theme days

Scripture Foundation (Optional)

"They will plant vineyards and eat their fruit."
— Amos 9:14

"The earth is the Lord's, and everything in it."
— Psalm 24:1

Sample Market Mission Statement

"We exist to nourish bodies, support local businesses, and strengthen community."

Bonus Ideas

Senior discount hour • Youth vendor booths • Faith & farming testimonies • Harvest festivals • Recipe handouts

The Sinner's Prayer

Father God,
I come to You in humility and truth.
I acknowledge that I have sinned and fallen
short of Your glory.
I cannot save myself, and I need Your mercy
and grace.

I believe that Jesus Christ is the Son of God.
I believe He lived a sinless life,
that He died on the cross for my sins,
and that He rose again on the third day,
victorious over sin and death.

Jesus, I confess You as my Lord and Savior.
I repent of my sins and turn away from my old
ways.
Wash me clean through Your precious blood.
Create in me a new heart and renew a right
spirit within me.

I receive Your forgiveness, Your salvation, and
Your eternal life.
From this day forward, I choose to follow You.
Teach me Your ways, lead me by Your Holy
Spirit,
and help me to live a life that brings glory to
God.

Thank You, Jesus, for saving me.
I receive this gift by faith, not by works.
I belong to You now.

In the name of Jesus Christ,
Amen.

What to Do After the Prayer

1. Believe What Has Just Happened

Salvation is a spiritual reality, not an emotional one.
Whether feelings change immediately or not, the truth remains:
you are forgiven, redeemed, and made new through Jesus Christ.

You are no longer defined by your past, your mistakes, or your shame.

2. Thank God Out Loud

Say a simple prayer of gratitude:

"Thank You, Father, for saving me.
Thank You for forgiving me.
Thank You that I belong to You."

Gratitude strengthens faith and anchors the heart in truth.

3. Begin Talking to God Daily

Prayer does not have to be formal or perfect.
Talk to God honestly—about fears, hopes,
questions, and needs.

You are not speaking to a distant judge,
but to a loving Father who listens.

4. Start Reading the Bible

Begin with:

The Gospel of John (to learn who Jesus is)

Psalms (for prayer and encouragement)

Romans (to understand salvation and grace)

Read slowly. Ask the Holy Spirit to teach you
as you read.

5. Turn Away From Old Patterns Gradually

Transformation is a process.
Some things may change quickly, others over
time.

When conviction comes, respond with
humility, not condemnation.
God corrects His children with love, not
shame.

6. Connect With Other Believers

Faith grows in community.
Seek fellowship with believers who encourage
truth, grace, and growth.

Healthy community strengthens obedience,
healing, and purpose.

7. Expect Growth, Not Perfection

You may stumble, but you are no longer lost.
When you fall, return to God immediately—do
not hide.

Grace is not permission to sin;
it is power to rise.

8. Declare This Truth

Say this aloud when needed:

"I am forgiven.
I am redeemed.
I belong to Jesus Christ.
My life now has purpose."

A Personal Prayer of Healing

Heavenly Father,
I come before You just as I am, in faith and humility. You are the Lord who heals me. You are the One who created my body, my soul, and my spirit, and nothing in me is hidden from You.

In the name of Jesus Christ, I receive Your healing power now.

Your Word says that Jesus bore my sicknesses and carried my pains, and by His stripes I am healed. I choose to believe Your Word over my symptoms, over fear, and over every report that does not agree with Your truth.

Father, I ask You to touch every part of my body—
every organ, every system, every cell, every bone, every muscle, and every nerve.
Where there has been pain, bring relief.
Where there has been weakness, release strength.
Where there has been inflammation, restore peace.
Where there has been damage, bring full restoration.

I ask for healing not only in my body, but in my soul.
Heal wounds caused by rejection, trauma, disappointment, grief, and loss.
Restore what has been broken by stress, shame, fear, or long seasons of waiting.
Let Your peace guard my heart and my mind.

Lord Jesus, You are the Prince of Peace. I receive Your peace now.
I release anxiety, heaviness, and emotional exhaustion.
I declare that my mind is renewed by the Word of God.
I have clarity, stability, and rest.

Holy Spirit, fill me from the top of my head to the soles of my feet.
Drive out every trace of infirmity, oppression, and weariness.
Let Your life flow through me like a river—bringing strength, balance, and renewal.

Father, I forgive everyone who has hurt me, disappointed me, or spoken against me.
I release bitterness and resentment.
I choose freedom.
I choose healing.
I choose life.

I declare over myself today:
I am not broken beyond repair.
I am not forgotten.
I am not too late.
I am not disqualified.

I am healed by the power of God.
I am being restored day by day.
My body responds to God's Word.
My strength is returning.
My hope is alive.